TH[...]

A prou[...]

Scandal has r[...]

Its glittering, gorgeous daughters are in disgrace.

Banished from the Balfour mansion, they're sent to the boldest, most magnificent men in the world to be wedded, bedded…and tamed!

And so begins a scandalous saga of dazzling glamour and passionate surrender.

**Each month, Harlequin Presents®
is delighted to bring you an exciting new
installment from THE BALFOUR BRIDES.
You won't want to miss out!**

MIA AND THE POWERFUL GREEK—
Michelle Reid

KAT AND THE DARE-DEVIL SPANIARD—
Sharon Kendrick

EMILY AND THE NOTORIOUS PRINCE—
India Grey

SOPHIE AND THE SCORCHING SICILIAN—
Kim Lawrence

ZOE AND THE TORMENTED TYCOON—
Kate Hewitt

ANNIE AND THE RED-HOT ITALIAN—
Carole Mortimer

BELLA AND THE MERCILESS SHEIKH—
Sarah Morgan

OLIVIA AND THE BILLIONAIRE CATTLE KING—
Margaret Way

Eight volumes to collect and treasure!

Just the sight of him rendered her fragile. In fact, she felt too shocked to move a muscle.

But the *eyes* were the eyes she remembered. Glowing and glittering like a full-grown African lion. She had no parallel for this. He hadn't looked like this in London or at the family wedding in Scotland. Then he had fit effortlessly into her world. But this was a far cry. Here in his own country he looked like a man who had never been tamed.

While she stared back in a kind of bemused horror, he put up his hand and swept off his hat in an extravagant gesture she interpreted as mocking. She could feel a blush further redden her face and neck. This was a dangerous man. Way outside her ken. And to think of it! She had put herself in his power.

Olivia did the only thing she could do.

She fainted.

Margaret Way

OLIVIA AND THE BILLIONAIRE CATTLE KING

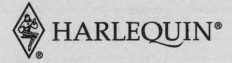

TORONTO • NEW YORK • LONDON
AMSTERDAM • PARIS • SYDNEY • HAMBURG
STOCKHOLM • ATHENS • TOKYO • MILAN • MADRID
PRAGUE • WARSAW • BUDAPEST • AUCKLAND

Recycling programs
for this product may
not exist in your area.

ISBN-13: 978-0-373-12976-8

OLIVIA AND THE BILLIONAIRE CATTLE KING

First North American Publication 2011

Copyright © 2010 by Harlequin Books S.A.

Special thanks and acknowledgment are given to Margaret Way for her contribution to The Balfour Brides series

All about the author...
Margaret Way

MARGARET WAY, a definite Leo, was born and raised in the subtropical river city of Brisbane, capital of Queensland, Australia, the Sunshine State. A conservatorium-trained pianist, teacher, accompanist and vocal coach, she found that her musical career came to an unexpected end when she took up writing—initially as a fun thing to do. She currently lives in a harborside apartment at beautiful Raby Bay, a thirty-minute drive from the state capital. She loves dining alfresco on her plant-filled balcony overlooking a translucent-green marina filled with all manner of pleasure craft—from motor cruisers costing millions of dollars and big, graceful yachts with carved masts standing tall against the cloudless blue sky, to little bay runabouts. No one and nothing is in a mad rush, and she finds the laid-back village atmosphere very conducive to her writing. With well over one hundred books to her credit, she still believes her best is yet to come.

PROLOGUE

I'M UP for the challenge. Of course I am! Nothing like a challenge to bring out the best in her. At the same time she was experiencing a definite sense of panic—the fear of finding herself in a strange land where she could conceivably be a lot unhappier than she already was?

You're not a Balfour for nothing, girl!

It was natural to her to talk to herself—a practice that had started very early in life. Maybe around seven, when she had found it hard to get attention. Still, she had grown up courageous—not too self-congratulatory a word, she fancied—and with a capacity for adjustment. Only these days her idea of herself had been badly shaken, something she didn't confide in everyone. Or she stopped herself in the nick of time.

She had always met her obligations, stood resolutely by her code of conduct which she firmly believed to be high, both in theory and in practise. Only problem now, she had lost her guiding star—her faith in herself—the ability she had always prided herself on to keep calm and in control. It was an ability she had learned the hard way, as surrogate mother to her siblings. Sadly that cherished ability had deserted her, bringing on her current sense of devastation. She who had always been such a stickler for doing the right thing had totally lost it. And boy did that hurt!

"Olivia, dear God!" Her father, the British billionaire, Oscar Balfour, using his steely blue eyes as a weapon, had reeled away from her in shock. "How could you? I just can't believe how you of all people have let me down."

Naturally a degree of resentment had erupted. Such criticism was hard to take after years of going all-out to please him.

Only the debacle wasn't just a bad dream. It had really occurred at the Balfour Charity Ball, instigated by her illustrious family a century before.

"The Balfour Ball has become an absolute must for anyone who is anyone in society." This from Great-aunt Edwina Balfour, the perfect upper-class snob. "On a par with an invitation to the palace."

Olivia could have responded she would throw over the Balfour Charity Ball any day for an invite to the palace, but had the great good sense not to. Nevertheless, the ball—the 100th no less— wasn't the occasion where one would have thought anyone in their right mind would get into a catfight. But that was exactly what she and her twin sister Bella had done that fateful night.

"And screw you!" Bella had tossed at her crudely, landing a stinging slap on her twin's cheek.

The silence thereafter had positively roared. Bella had never struck her, but the incident was now indelibly printed on their memories, possibly for a lifetime. Such a serious breach of etiquette was rarer than rare. Betrayal of family was not to be condoned. The only mitigating circumstance was both she and Bella had meant well. Their argument was all about the fate and future of their much-loved sibling Zoe.

Poor Zoe!

So there they were on that night of nights, all dressed to the nines, beautiful formal gowns and magnificent family heirloom jewellery, except for Bella, who always liked to be different, more daring, setting trends with avant-garde labels and loads of costume glitter. She, Olivia, the sensible, practical—might as well say it—*sanctimonious* one, the eldest of the "Beautiful Balfour Girls," pitted against the highly volatile, sparkling Bella, who in retrospect could be judged as the one having the most heart. She could no longer blind herself to that telling fact.

Having laid all her cards on the table she recognised that, as much as she loved and cherished her twin, she had always been inclined to patronise Bella, regarding her sister as someone who, though very beautiful, perhaps lacked intellectual depth. Bella didn't read books or ponder issues as she did. Bella had not completed her university degree as she had to some distinction. Bella had no great interest in the arts generally.

Their tastes weren't the same. In fact, they were opposites. Bella played up her stunning beauty. Olivia deliberately played hers down. They weren't identical twins, but fraternal. Bella closely resembled their dead mother, the exquisite Alexandra. Bella was more the Balfour, with the Balfour blue eyes.

Olivia was far more responsible than her twin. Bella was the first to admit that. She didn't have Bella's kind of freedom. Bella's sole interest was to have a good time, leaving her, the elder by a few minutes, to toe the line. It was Olivia who often acted as her father's hostess, kept up the Balfour charity work, supervised and instructed when necessary her younger siblings—her half-sisters—coped with their dependency on her, while Bella led her glamorous, very hectic social life always pursued by a conga line of admirers.

Be that as it may, their calamitous fight had been their only real argument.

"As twins we stick together! One for all and all for one!" This was their childhood swashbuckling mantra when they were heavily into Alexandre Dumas. She and Bella loved each other. They loved Zoe, who as it turned out was not their father's child, but their late mother's indiscretion. Their *mother* of all people! She, who they had regarded as being right up there with Mother Teresa.

"Mother must have been a saint. They say only the good die young." She had actually said that once to Bella in an effort to curb her sister's wildness, which went far beyond high spirits. Both of them at the time had believed it to be entirely true.

Now she had to pinch herself hard to remind herself that darling Zoe was therefore illegitimate. She and Bella had argued over whether to tell Zoe or conceal the fact from her. Their fiery debate had had devastating consequences for the entire family.

"If only I could go back in time!" She often found herself breaking the silence to lament. They hadn't been foolish enough to conduct their argument in public. They had had the sense to retire to a private room to hurl insults at each other, but not the continuing good sense to shut the door firmly. Their heated discussion over Zoe's legitimacy, a matter that consumed them, had been overheard by an unscrupulous member of the press.

The press and the paparazzi were forever hot on the trail of the Beautiful Balfour Girls, Bella in particular. The journalist must have thought all his coups had come at once. He got off a starkly telling photo of the two of them in the heat of their fury—hers self-righteous, Bella's impassioned—plus all he had overheard of their argument which was practically verbatim. Next morning, story and photograph had been splashed across the front page of a national newspaper.

Another Illegitimacy Scandal Rocks Balfour Family

Even as she thought of it Olivia cringed in mind and body. When would the soul-searching stop? When would her disgust with herself begin to abate? She had to face the fact she could be left with eternal regret or, as Bella had said lying limply across her twin's bed, "Sooner or later, Olivia, we have to pay for our sins. When it comes down to it we're no different from anyone else."

What nonsense! Of course they were different. They lived in a stately home for one thing. The family was mentioned in *Debrett's* and *Who's Who*. To top it off their father was a billionaire. This time they were *all* paying, from her illustrious father down, when it was she and Bella who had finally toppled the grand Balfour edifice. How shocking was that?

Was it any wonder their father had reinstituted the Balfour Family Rules, a code of conduct that had been passed down from generation to generation within the Balfour family? All eight of Oscar's daughters through their father's three marriages, and both their mother's and their father's misalliances—had accepted his decision to send them away from the scene of the family humiliation.

"You need to face your limitations, my daughters, and hopefully find your strengths," he had exhorted with as much gravitas as a hanging judge.

They could have refused. She had certainly considered it. But they didn't.

"A point very much in your favour," Oscar Balfour conceded.

Bella had been handed rule one. Dignity.

She had been given her own rule. Rule eight. Humility.

When their father had first handed her rule eight, she had looked back at him in blank astonishment.

"Humility, Daddy? What can you mean?" She felt enormously hurt.

He had taken up valuable time to explain.

Now in a moment of self-clarity she saw she just *might* have a need to develop that overrated virtue. She knew what people thought of her: aloof, cool to the point of glacial, supremely self-confident, self-assured, really a snob and a bit of a prude, the least approachable of the Balfour girls. Not true. At least, not entirely. The *cool* bit was in order. She was a private person. Indeed she had a passion for privacy. But at the heart of it she couldn't do without her defence mechanisms any more than Bella, both of them cruelly robbed of a mother and a mother's love and guidance when they had barely mastered the trick of abseiling down their cots.

"Doesn't anyone realise what losing a mother does to a child? The effects are felt forever."

"God, tell me something I don't know!" Bella, clad in a gorgeous imperial-yellow silk kimono decorated with richly embroidered chrysanthemums and mystical birds, had cried. In many ways Bella was a bit of a drama queen.

So in the end she and Bella, who really didn't have a personality disorder as she had so wrongly accused her, accepted their banishments.

"Both of us have to master the rule, Olivia." Bella, for once, showed meekness.

It was certainly their father's directive. A cue for obedience if ever there was one. "It will get you safely through life so you never again bring shame on the family name." He had spoken as if he was throwing them all a lifeline. For herself, she had to confess she ever so slightly resented the fact he had omitted to mention his own part in the debacle. It was his "girls" who had to take the direct hit.

"We have to work out our punishment," Bella had said, apparently not feeling the same degree of betrayal. "Take it on the chin."

"Punishment? I prefer to look on it as a challenge."

A challenge—far, far away from their comfort zone.

"Good grief, Daddy, not Australia!" She had a vision of that very large island continent not all that far off the South Pole. Surely they had sent convicts there?

"Australia, it is!" Her father had fixed her with the piercing Balfour eyes. "You're to work in whatever capacity is required of you, Olivia. At least you have the Balfour good business head on your shoulders."

She should have reminded him that had already been established. But to be obliged to work for a man she had only met briefly and had cause to intensely dislike? Could she even do it, much as she was made of stern stuff?

Clint McAlpine, Australian cattle baron, had been the only person in her life outside Bella who had had the temerity to tell her to her face—she had only been showing him her *normal* demeanour at the time—that she badly needed taking down a peg.

"Come down from your high ivory tower, ice princess," he'd advised, a satirical twist to his handsome mouth. "Mix with mere mortals. I promise it will do you a power of good."

She winced at the memory! Just because he was a billionaire like their father didn't give him the right to tick her off. Maybe for that very reason his image, incredibly vivid, had stuck in her head. It had never diminished. Something she didn't understand.

There was some distant family connection on her father's side; that's how they had met up. Functions, a family wedding. The McAlpines often visited London on business or pleasure or a mix of both. A few years back, her father had bought a large block of shares in the McAlpine Pastoral Company which must have prompted his decision to send her into the McAlpine stronghold. Evidently her father trusted McAlpine as he had trusted McAlpine's late father, a man of good British stock. He must have been a much nicer man altogether. So now, a scant two days after the Balfour *disaster* she was on the threshold of taking up her challenge.

At the end of the earth.

Australia.

CHAPTER ONE

*Darwin, capital of the Northern Territory,
gateway to Australia*

NEVER a good traveller—her privileged lifestyle had ensured a great deal of international jet-setting—Olivia had come to the conclusion this had to be the epic journey of all time. First there was the flight from London to Singapore. Horrendous! Well over fourteen hours of claustrophobia. She had tried, largely in vain, to gather her resources with a one-night stopover at Raffles. Lovely hotel with a unique charm. She fully intended to revisit it at some future date, but for now on to Darwin, the tropical capital of the Northern Territory of Australia, yet another four and more hours away.

She couldn't read. She couldn't sleep. All she could do was dwell on her disastrous fall from grace. She knew she had no alternative but to fight back. And not take an age about it either. She and her siblings were due back in London five months hence to celebrate their father's birthday on October 2. Nothing for it but to pull up her socks! Re-establish her aristocratic credentials.

Could be hard going in Australia.

Looking wanly out the aircraft porthole she could see the glitter of the Timor Sea. It was a genuine turquoise. That aroused her interest sufficiently to make her sit up and take notice. They continued their descent, and Darwin City's skyline rose up.

Skyline! Good grief!

She craned her neck nearer the porthole. After London, New

York and the great cities of Europe, all of which she had visited, it looked more like something out of a Somerset Maugham novel—a tropical outpost, as it were. It was bound to be sweltering. She knew the heat of the Caribbean where her father owned a beautiful private island, but she had a premonition the heat of Darwin was going to be something else again. And she the one who had often been described as the "quintessential English rose"! Anyone who knew the slightest thing about gardening would know roses hated extreme heat.

Yet her father had sent her here and she had obeyed his decision. But then hadn't she obeyed him all of her life? Struggling to always be what he wanted, while Bella was out enjoying herself, men falling around her like ninepins.

"Only flings, sweetie! Something to get me through a desperately dull life."

She had thanked Bella for sharing that with her. Far from being the quintessential English rose she was starting to think of herself as the quintessential old maid who, far from bedding lovers, burnt gallons of midnight oil reading profound and often obscure literature. She even dressed like a woman ten years her senior. Or so Bella said. How had *that* developed? Her father's fault for expecting way too much of her, especially from an early age. Bella's taunt aside, she thought she always looked impeccably groomed—that was her duty—but she saw now with her perfect up-do, her whole style could be too much on the conservative side for a woman of twenty-eight.

Twenty-eight! My God, when was she going to start the breeding process? Time was running out. Bella had had dozens of affairs and countless proposals. She'd had exactly two. Both perfect disasters. Geoffrey, then Justin. They had only wanted her because she was her father's daughter. Bella's men wanted just Bella. Wasn't that a bit of a sore point? But could she blame them? Bella was everything she was not: sexy, exciting, daring, adventurous, not afraid to show lots of creamy cleavage, whereas she was as modest as a novice nun. She could see herself now as being as dull as ditch water. That image bruised her ego. Or what was left of it.

What would she make of Australia? The Northern Territory she understood was pretty much one sprawling wilderness area. She hadn't *wanted* Australia. Too hot and primitive. But in the end she had accepted the commitment. She was a Balfour, British to the bone.

Darwin City. *City?* She could see a township built on a bluff at the edge of a peninsula surrounded on three sides by sparkling blue-green water. It overlooked what appeared to be a very large harbour. Being her, she had made it her business to read up on the place so she knew the city had been destroyed and rebuilt twice. Once after the massive Japanese air raid in February 1942 during World War II, when more bombs were dropped on an un-prepared Darwin than had been dropped on Pearl Harbor. Then again after the city was destroyed by a terrifying natural disaster, Cyclone Tracy, in 1974. She rather thought after something as cataclysmic as that she would pack up her things and move to the Snowy Mountains, but apparently the people of the Top End were a lot tougher than she.

She well remembered McAlpine as projecting a powerful image: tough, aggressive, a man's man, but women seemed to adore him. It was a wonder his body didn't glow with the force of that exuberant energy. Not that he wasn't a cultured man in his way. Rather he projected a dual image. The rough, tough cattle baron with an abrasive tongue, and the highly regarded chair-man and CEO of M.A.P.C., the McAlpine Pastoral Company. Her billionaire businessman father wouldn't have bought into the company otherwise.

Much as she loved and respected her father she realised there was some ambivalence in her towards him. He hadn't been what she and Bella had wanted. A doting, hands-on dad. Their father, always in pursuit of even more power and money—throw in women—hadn't been around for his daughters most of the time. In a sense that had left her and Bella, in particular, orphans, mere babes in the woods. She had detected the same kind of brilliance and that certain ruthlessness in McAlpine.

Her father had worked his way through three wives, a catastrophic one-night stand and more than likely a number of affairs they didn't know about. She chose to ignore the fact that her and Bella's mother, Alexandra, had cheated on him—who knows for what reason? Might have been a good one. Their mother was their mother after all. They had wanted their memory of her to remain sacred. Ah, well! Sooner or later one had to face the realities of life.

She knew of McAlpine's marriage to an Australian heiress with an unusual name. It had ended in an acrimonious divorce. She wasn't in the least surprised. He was that kind of man. Probably he had treated his ex-wife badly, had affairs. There was a young daughter, she seemed to recall, who no doubt would have been swiftly dispatched to her mother to look after. One couldn't expect a tycoon to work out a little girl's problems. She and Bella hadn't enjoyed much of their father's attention or problem solving.

With an effort she shook herself out of what Bella liked to call "Your martyr mode, darling! There it is again!" She didn't recognise it herself. She was no martyr even if she was practically a saint with the weight of the world on her shoulders.

She had noted the cattle baron was big on sex appeal. Something women drooled over. He was devilishly handsome. In her view in an overtly sexy way. But she had to concede *real* sexual presence. She was prepared to grant him that but she, for one, had had no trouble combating it. Such men shrieked a warning to a discerning woman like herself. She preferred far more subtle English good looks and style—like Justin's, even if he had turned out to be an appalling cad. Bella had called him a "love rat." She couldn't see McAlpine as a *rat*. But then what did she know? She, who appeared to be incapable of one lasting relationship with a man.

What she did know was, she neither trusted nor liked McAlpine. She didn't doubt her ability to keep him in his place.

She was a Balfour after all. A sensible, stable person who had never required being kept an eye on. Maybe she had blotted her near-perfect copybook, but she'd had the grace to accuse herself of her failures. Her task now was to regain her self-esteem and emerge as a more nurturing, more compassionate, more liberal-minded person willing and able to accept advice.

But not from McAlpine.

Inside Darwin International Airport she looked around her in disbelief. Was Darwin a beach resort? The atmosphere was torrid even for May when it surely should have been cooling down. The hot humid air was fitfully swept by cooling breezes off the harbour. Overhead domed a burning blue sky. Northern Hemisphere skies didn't have that intensity of colour. Soaring coconut palms and spreading flamboyant trees were everywhere. She had to wonder if ever a stray coconut fell on some unfortunate head. She supposed one could always sue.

The vegetation was rampantly tropical, full of strong primary colours that assaulted the eye, the air saturated with strange fragrances. Sunlight streamed down in bars of molten gold. As for the quality of the light! Even with her sunglasses on her eyes were dazzled. So much so in the middle of her ruminations she nearly collided with someone.

"I'm so sorry." She was tempted to tell the man who had accosted her he couldn't have been watching where he was going.

"No worries, love."

She registered in amazement his incredible outfit. Navy boxer shorts with a frog-green singlet.

"You need help, little lady?"

That, when she was some inches taller than he. She momentarily closed her eyes. "I'm fine, thank you. Someone will be meeting me."

"Lucky devil!"

Olivia's Balfour blue eyes glinted. Why did it have to be a man? She could have been meeting a favourite aunt. She continued making slow progress through the swirling throng, marvelling at the sights around her.

She had never seen such flimsy dressing in her entire life, nor so much bare skin. Not even on the Caribbean islands. Nor so many marvellously attractive children, girls and exotic young women with startlingly beautiful black eyes, and skin either gilded honey, café au lait, light fawn or chocolate. They were all petite, with lovely slender limbs. Not for the first time in her life she felt like a giraffe, more pallid than she really was. Even Bella might have a job being singled out here. She didn't know if these people were part aboriginal, part Indonesian, part New Guinean, part Chinese—anywhere from South-East Asia.

She didn't know this part of the world at all. But they were all Australians, it seemed. They spoke with the same distinctive Australian accent, so much broader than her own and—it had to be said—the voices so much *louder*. No comment seemed to be offered quietly. She recalled her own voice had often been referred to as "cut glass." But then they all spoke like that, the Balfours.

Heavens, was it possible she was a snob after all? For a moment she wondered if she had caught herself out. Looking around her she saw Australia's proximity to Asia was well in evidence. This was a melting pot. Fifty nationalities made up the one-hundred-thousand-strong population and they all seemed to be waiting for flights out or meeting up with relatives and friends. She remembered now Darwin was the base for tourists who wanted to explore the World Heritage–listed Kakadu National Park and the great wilderness areas of Arnhem Land. She could readily believe such areas would be magnificent, but she couldn't think how they would find the strength to go exploring in such *heat*!

She hadn't thought to take off her long-sleeved Armani jacket. No chance of her ever getting about in floral bras, halter necks and short shorts like the young women around her. Not that there was anything wrong with her legs. Or her arms. Any part of her body for that matter. The jacket she wore over a slim skirt and a cream silk shirt beneath. Now she wished she had taken off the jacket. She was *melting* with little chance to mop her brow. The humid heat was far beyond anything she was used to. By Darwin standards she realised she was ridiculously overdressed. Absolutely nobody looked like her. Even her expensive shoes felt damp and clonky.

She was fully aware of all the curious glances directed her way. She also had quite a number of pieces of luggage to be off-loaded—all necessary, all bearing the famous Louis Vuitton label. Now she wished she had bought some ordinary everyday luggage. It was starkly apparent she didn't fit in. Worse, she must have looked helpless.

"All right, love, are you?"

Olivia turned, astonished. Obviously she did have *helpless* or *hopeless* tattooed on her brow. For out of the milling crowd had emerged a pretty dark-skinned woman somewhere in her thirties, a little pudgy around the tummy, wearing a loose, floral dress alight with beautiful hand-painted hibiscus and some kind of rubber flip-flops on her feet. Despite that Olivia could see with her trained eyes that this was a woman of consequence, albeit in her own way. She had that certain look Olivia recognised, the self-assurance in the fathomless black eyes. She also wore a look of kindly concern. Olivia valued concern and kindness. Olivia liked her immediately. Something that happened rarely with strangers.

"Thank you for asking, but I'm quite all right."

"Don't look it, love!" The woman flashed a smile, still observing Olivia closely.

Did all these people speak their thoughts aloud? Olivia felt giddy and terribly overheated, as though the sun had bored a hole in her skull.

"Yah pale, and that lovely porcelain face of yours is flushed and covered in sweat. What say we sit down for a moment, love." She paused to look around her. "Long flight, was it? You're a Pom, of course. No mistakin' the accent." The woman laughed softly. "No offence, love. Me great-grandad was a Pom. Sent out to oversee the Pommy pearling interest. Used to be big in those days. His family never acknowledged me but that's OK. I never acknowledged 'im. So come on." She took Olivia's nerveless arm in a motherly fashion. "Over here. Don't want you faintin' on us."

Olivia's laugh was brittle. "I've never fainted in my life." Nevertheless she allowed herself to be led away.

"Always a first time, love. They reckon five out of ten people faint at some point of their life. I fainted when I got speared one time. Accident, o' course, but I nearly died. Me and Rani were out fishin' for barra—that's barramundi, if you don't know. Best-eatin' fish in the world."

"I have heard of it," Olivia said, not wanting to be impolite. "It's terribly *hot*, isn't it?" She sank rather feebly onto one of the long bench seats arranged in rows.

"This is cool for us, love. By the sound of it you wouldn't want to be here in the wet. It's just over." The woman took a seat beside her. "What are you doin' here anyway? Don't look like a tourist to me. Look more like the wind blow you in, the wind blow you out. A bit spooky!"

"Spooky?" Olivia felt what was left of her self-confidence ooze away.

"Something about you, love." The woman looked searchingly into Olivia's blue eyes. "Your spirit bin wounded. Somethin' happened you weren't countin' on? Don't worry, yah spirit will heal here, far, far away from what you left behind. You're gunna be able to display your *real* colours."

Olivia, who fancied she had something of a gift, recognised a prophecy when she heard one. "Oh, I hope so!" The strange woman continued to stare directly into her eyes. Just as hypnotists do. Probably she *was* one. Or a sorceress. Then again she might discover the woman wasn't real.

"Yah bin like a bird in a cage strugglin' to escape," the woman continued, her tone at lullaby pitch. "Beatin' yah wings and flingin' yourself against the bars. You have to have the *will* to escape."

"Maybe I've been frightened to fly alone?" Incredibly Oliva found herself divulging that startling piece of information.

"Escape is within reach."

The one thing she hadn't reckoned on was an airport clairvoy-ant. "I'm waiting for a Mr Clint McAlpine to pick me up," she confided in another strange burst of friendliness. "I'm to work for him."

It was the woman's turn to be astonished. "Clint hired yah?"

"You call him Clint?" Olivia was somewhat taken aback. No one, for instance, outside of family and close friends called her father Oscar. Dear me, no!

"Now, now, love, don't come over the Pom." The woman tapped her hand lightly. "We all call him Clint. We love him up here. He's the best fella in the world. A fittin' heir for his dad, who's up there in the Milky Way, the home of the Great Beings and our ancestors. I'm Bessie Malgil, by the way. I shoulda told yah. Everyone knows me around here. I paint."

"Pictures?" Olivia stared at her with quickening interest.

"Not *your* kind of pictures, love. We're talkin' indigenous art. Now how about you? What's your name? Lady Somethin', I'll be bound!"

"Olivia Balfour." Olivia gave the Good Samaritan her hand. "No title."

"Don't need one. Written all over yah. Nice to meet yah, Livvy," Bessie said, giving Olivia's elegant long-fingered hand a gentle shake.

Livvy! She had waited all her life to be called Livvy.

"My golly, girl, you've taken on a challenge comin' down here to this part of the world. You look like you belong in one of them fine palaces."

"No, Bessie, no!" Olivia shook her head, a movement that only increased her dizziness. "I'm just an ordinary person but I am interested in challenges."

"Not today you ain't!" Bessie pronounced firmly. "Look, love, let's get you out of that straitjacket. Not that it ain't dressy but we need to make a start. You're overheatin', that's for sure. Clint's comin', yah say?"

"Oh, I do hope so." Olivia rose in a rather wobbly fashion to her feet, while Bessie helped her out of her linen jacket, folding it neatly over the back of the bench.

"If he said he bin here, he'll bin here," Bessie stated with the utmost faith. "Blow me down if that's not 'im coming now!" Her whole face lit up. "Bin out on a muster by the look of it." She chuckled. "Last week he was sellin' two of the Queensland stations in the chain. People are lookin' for cheaper beef. Global recession an' all. We can deliver better up here in the Territory. Your worries are over, Livvy. Here he comes."

Olivia started to her feet again, for once in her life standing awkwardly. McAlpine was coming. From where? What direction? Even as her eyes swept the crowded terminal she became aware of a ripple of pleasure, of recognition and excitement, in the crowd. She even detected a sprinkle of clapping. Something that always happened when royalty was around.

Bessie's indicating hand came up. "Here he is, love. Right on time."

Olivia followed her gaze helplessly. McAlpine?

All she could see was a strikingly tall, *wild*-looking man striding towards them. Some character that embodied the great outdoors, or the hero of a big-budget adventure movie set in the desert sands of Arabia or the jungles of the Amazon, the ones she avoided. This man was dressed in what she took to be the ultimate in bush gear. Khaki shirt, khaki trousers, a surprisingly fancy silver buckle on the leather belt he had slung around his lean waist. Polished high-heeled cowboy boots made him even taller than he already was. A wide-brimmed cream hat, the Australian slouch hat, was set at a rakish angle on his head. His hair, a dark auburn in colour, was almost long enough to pull into a ponytail, for God's sake! When had he last visited a hairdresser? Most of his darkly tanned face was covered by thick stubble that, left another few days, could turn into a full beard.

Just the sight of him rendered her fragile. In fact, she felt too shocked to move a muscle.

But the *eyes* were the eyes she remembered. Glowing and glittering like a full-grown African lion. She had no parallel for this. He hadn't looked like this in London or at the family wedding in Scotland. Then he had fitted effortlessly into her world. But this was a far cry. Here in his own country he looked like a man who had never been tamed.

While she stared back in a kind of bemused horror, he suddenly put up his hand and swept off his wide-brimmed slouch hat in an extravagant gesture she interpreted as mocking. He looked quite *extraordinary*! A totally different breed. She could feel a blush further redden her face and neck. This was a dangerous man. Way outside her ken. And to think of it! She had put herself in his power.

Olivia did the only thing she could do.

She fainted.

A lot of things had happened to him in his eventful thirty-eight years, but he had never had a woman collapse in a dead faint into his arms. A beautiful woman no less—tall, elegant, with classic aristocratic features. His mind was suddenly filled with his irritating but surprisingly vivid memories of her. Olivia Balfour, ice princess, had only just arrived and already she was trouble.

"Poor little thing!" Bessie crooned, as he swiftly fielded the young English woman's tall, too-slender body, lowering her so she lay flat along the empty bench.

"She'd be all of five-eight in her bare feet," he pointed out drily.

"Yeah, but she looks kinda vunerable, don't you think?"

"*Vul*nerable, Bessie," McAlpine corrected, privately agreeing.

"Whatever!" Bessie shrugged. "I always say vunerable. Why don't you never tell me before?"

"Never heard you say it, but you're spot on."

"'Course I am. Anyway, knew this was gunna happen. Too

many clothes. I spotted that right off." She leaned over to slip off Olivia's low-heeled, very expensive leather shoes.

"Who wouldn't?" McAlpine commented drily. He seemed to remember telling the high-and-mighty Ms Olivia Balfour to get off her high horse, pedestal, whatever. She had got under his skin and he hadn't bothered to hide it. The divorce coming up. That was his excuse. Marigole had been giving him all the flack she could muster.

"Not used to our heat," Bessie was saying. "How she's gunna survive outback, boss, I dunno as yet."

"It'll come to you, Bessie, like it always does. You and I both know lilies thrive." He stared down at Ms Balfour's still, lily-skinned face. She had very long eyelashes. They were starting to flutter. A good sign. He moved his hand to undo a few buttons on her silk shirt. She had done it up almost to the neck despite the pressing heat which today was climbing to near forty degrees Celsius. Did she have no sense at all? Next he slipped the waist button on her tight pencil-slim skirt. "Cold water, Bessie, chop, chop."

"Sure, boss!" Bessie spun on her thongs to obey, just as a terminal staff member hurried towards them, a very attractive brunette who had waited her moment to zoom over to them, physically beating off another female attendant in the process. She carried a plastic container of ice-cold water.

"Is she all right?" the brunette enquired, looking not at the faint victim as perhaps she should have, but full into the cattle baron's extraordinary big-cat topaz eyes. They were stunning in his bronze face. She had been told he was a hunk. She wasn't at all disappointed. Hunk was too tame. He was drop-dead *gorgeous*!

"She's coming around." Clint frowned slightly, taking Olivia's pulse. A bit rapid but not overly weak. "Thanks for that." He took the container from the attendant without really seeing her.

"No problem, Mr McAlpine." Long heavily mascaraed eyelashes batted away, her fingers tingling deliciously from the brief contact with his. Gosh, he was awesome! And he was unattached.

Everyone in the Territory knew his marriage hadn't worked out. Unbelievable! The ex-wife had to be a blend of near blind and mentally challenged. "Could she need medical attention?" she asked helpfully. "I can arrange it."

"I shouldn't think so." Gently Clint tapped Olivia Balfour's cheeks. They were cool and damp and not worryingly hot and dry. "She's exhausted from the long flight and she's overdressed. The cold water will cool her down." He realised after a moment the brunette was lingering on. He had got used to this kind of thing. Women worked hard at attracting him, often outrageously. Amazing how much more attractive having money made a man. "Thank you." He gave her a smile that held a pleasant dismissal and reluctantly the airline attendant tore herself away, heading back to her mundane duties.

Olivia opened her eyes, trying desperately to reorientate herself.

Dear God, had she died and been transported to hell or what passed for it? She made a grab for someone's shirt. Heat was swirling all around her. Surely she didn't deserve *this*?

Full consciousness swiftly returned. She was looking straight into McAlpine's lion's eyes. She uncurled her fingers which were twined like tentacles of a vine around his arm. "God help me, did I faint?"

"Ah, the princess awakens from her slumbers!" he murmured suavely. "God help you, you *did*, Ms Balfour." He rose to his impressive height. "Look, I'm going to lift you so your head is resting back against my shoulder. Then I want you to drink some cold water. Bessie will help."

"Oh, good, Bessie…" She was enormously grateful Bessie, her Good Samaritan, hadn't left her.

"I'm here, love, don't you worry." Bessie, who had already decided to take this beautiful, fragile lady under her wing, had moved in close, clucking like a mother hen. Why, the willowy creature had eyes as blue as a Ulysses butterfly's wing and skin so white she might have been zoomed down from a celestial planet. Bessie took the container in hand.

"Really, I'm all right!" Olivia protested, when she felt like a rag mop.

"*Really*, you aren't," McAlpine drawled. He sat behind her, drawing her upper body against him. Immediately she slumped her golden head gratefully against his shoulder, clearly needing assistance. She might be terribly hot and bothered, he thought, but her skin gave off the most exquisite scent of roses. "Right, Bessie. Let's get it into her."

"Always wanted to be a nurse." Bessie chuckled. "Like takin' care of people."

"Well, now's your chance."

"She's lucky I sensed her," Bessie said with satisfaction. "Not that me antennae bin flyin' solo. The crowd had spotted her too. Never seen anyone so beatific in their whole lives."

"*Beatific?*" Clint laughed. "That's a good word, Bess."

"Means angel, don't it?"

"Looking like an angel."

"Or mebbe a brolga in search of water. Jes' standin' there, she was."

Brolga? Olivia felt a wash of panic. What was a brolga, for heaven's sake? Some sort of slang for bird brain?

McAlpine's body was disturbingly hot, hard and steely strong, the sweat on him clean—an arresting combination of pheromones and the vast outdoors, dead sexy in its way. For an insane moment she wondered what it would be like to know that body intimately. The next she wondered if it were possible she was on the verge of a spectacular mental breakdown. She had only set foot on this tropical outpost and already she was going troppo. She knew the term. Surely some Englishman who had spent too long in the tropics had invented it? She had never thought to experience it firsthand.

"Relax, no one is going to hurt you," McAlpine said, as though humouring a fractious filly. "You need to cool down."

"You're gunna be OK, love." Bessie gave her a big comforting smile, putting the plastic container to Olivia's lips.

It was *sooo* good! Nothing in the world could have tasted better than pure cold water.

"Sip it," McAlpine cautioned. "Don't gulp."

Even physically reduced, she bridled. "Hang on. I'm *not*—"

"Sip it," he repeated, with a grimace of impatience.

Feeling childish, she slowly finished off the container of water, becoming aware she was the centre of attention. "Please, I can sit up."

"Sure you can." He was already in the process of helping her sit straight. Even with that loose wave of hair falling across her cheek, her shirt in slight disarray, the button of her skirt undone, she still managed to look elegant. No mean feat.

"How do you feel now?" Her eyes were the *exact* colour of the beautiful blue glaze on a Sung Dynasty vase at the house.

"Everyone is staring at me," Olivia said worriedly. And so they were. Not rudely but sympathetically. She was sure the news had got about. *The blonde lady fainted. A Pom.* That explained it. Why wouldn't she in the unaccustomed heat? The good news was she had Clint McAlpine, the Territory's biggest cattle baron, to look out for her. The man might have been a national icon.

"How do you know they're not staring at *me*?" he countered, watching yet another silky swathe of her beautiful blonde hair fall from her impeccable up-do. The few times he had seen her she'd always had her long hair pulled back tightly from her face and fashioned into some kind of knot. This was one repressed female. It would probably take a surgical team to get her out of her suit.

"So humiliating to faint!" Olivia murmured in embarrassment, as though it was on a par with jumping off a bridge only to land unhurt knee-deep in mud.

"Don't be ridiculous." He was pleased to see a little of her colour had come back, warming her flawless skin. The fact her father had wanted to send her out to Australia, and to him in particular, had come as quite a shock and he didn't shock easily. He knew about the scandal, of course. Even if it hadn't made their newspapers, he had plenty of relatives, friends and contacts in the UK only too pleased to pass on the gossip. Frankly he couldn't see her getting into a punch-up with her beautiful sister, the so-called "wild one." Olivia was the ice princess, unwilling and seemingly unable to leave her marble pedestal. But for once she had lost it. From what little he knew of her she would be smarting badly.

He knew she needed a good long sleep. As a seasoned traveller—he was aware of her jet-setting—he had thought she would take the last leg of her flight from Singapore to Darwin in her stride. He knew she had made an overnight stay at Raffles. Only the best for Ms Balfour. He couldn't chance flying her to the station. Not today. Another overnight stay was called for. He could take her to the harbourside apartment the family maintained. McAlpine money had built the luxury complex. Or perhaps it would be advisable to book them into the Darwin International Resort Hotel. It was only a short distance away.

On the face of it Ms Balfour didn't seem right for any job he could easily set her. Probably she had never been inside a kitchen in her entire life. Not that any of the McAlpine operations needed a cook—even if he could send a woman like her to an outstation. Out of the question. He had Kath and Norm Cartwright, husband-and-wife team, running domestic affairs at Kalla Koori.

Maybe Ms Balfour couldn't cook, or keep house, and she sure as hell wouldn't be able to tackle the hardest game of all, mustering cattle, but she looked far from stupid. In fact, she looked highly intelligent. As she would have to be.

He knew she had often acted as her father's hostess and done the usual things for a young woman in her privileged position: charity work, opening fetes and nursing homes, that kind of thing. If she could cut the swanning around bit, she would be quite an asset to him on the social side of things. He had functions to give, important guests to entertain. He fancied Ms Balfour would find acting organiser and hostess a piece of cake.

She would, however, have to lighten up on the upper-crust hauteur. He seemed to remember he had told her, among other things, she had elevated snobbery to an art form. Ouch! He could hardly expect her to like him any more than he liked her.

Yet she was here. Oscar Balfour had sent her. Oscar Balfour was a good man to have onside. His late father had liked the man immensely. Oscar Balfour did have patrician good looks and a great deal of charm. Also a great deal of money. Oscar Balfour was a significant shareholder in M.A.P.C. It followed that both of them, he and Ms Balfour, would have to make the best of things or kill off each other in the process.

CHAPTER TWO

MCALPINE had to be a celebrity.

Everywhere they went he was waved at, smiled at, greeted with a mix of awe, respect and enthusiastic friendliness. He could have been a rock star in town for a huge open-air concert.

Overnight the stubble had disappeared. Morning found him clean-shaven but still with that "wild man" look, ensuring women never took their eyes off him. She was sure what she was registering was plain primal lust. She didn't know whether to feel disgusted or deprived. She had never seen anything like the combination of his thick, lustrous dark auburn hair, bronze skin— she'd never seen a tan richer, darker— and confronting golden eyes. He had even found time to have his hair trimmed. One couldn't have said "cut." No regimental short back and sides. Oh, well, it was beautiful hair after all. Most women would give up a valuable eye tooth to have hair like it.

Why couldn't the man have been *ordinary*? A good twenty years older? A father figure. Even uncle figure would have done. Her father's choice of McAlpine was the worst of the worst. They had absolutely nothing in common. Even more upsetting was the fact they were basically hostile to each other. He certainly brought out the offensive in her. She was good for a joust. If one wanted peace, one prepared for war. But then again, war wasn't good when she had to work for the man, and he no doubt would be reporting back to her father.

There was *one* good thing, however. She had slept like the proverbial log. And he had let her. Until 9:00 a.m., that is, when he had called her hotel room to instruct her to come down for breakfast without delay, after which they were flying on. At least he had had the decency to enquire whether she had slept at all.

"Thank you for asking about the quality of my sleep." She willed herself to be cool. Not easy when there was some extraordinary *heat* at her centre. "I slept very well, Mr McAlpine." Even as she answered she had thrown back the light bedclothes and leapt to her feet. "I hope you weren't worrying about me?" She couldn't prevent the note of sarcasm in her voice.

"Not in the least, Ms Balfour. But it's time to put a little pressure on you. I'm sure being a Balfour you're up for it. We'll have breakfast—I've already taken the liberty of ordering—then we must be on our way. Business beckons. I'm sure you're well used to that kind of thing from your father. See you in the foyer."

She had showered, dressed and was downstairs in under twenty minutes, a positive record for her. Unfortunately she hadn't had time to arrange her hair in its customary neat pleat. She had to knot the billowy blonde masses with a gold clasp at the nape. The foyer was surprisingly busy, people going back and forth, all acting happy to be there. No sign of McAlpine; he had to be dead easy to spot with his looks and height. But no, he was nowhere about. No fan groups circling in tight knots.

"Ms Balfour, I presume."

"Oh, I'm *so* sorry!" She actually backed into him. Or had he let her? She spun, acutely embarrassed, feeling the crescendo of heat that arose from his hands momentarily on her shoulders. A light pressure actually, yet she felt it right down to her toes. They instantly turned up.

"Let's go in, shall we?" he suggested suavely.

He was appraising her with faint incredulity, as though she was made of strawberries and whipped cream, Olivia thought crossly. "It might have been an idea to meet up inside the restaurant," she pointed out loftily, regaining her habitual cool.

"So what are you saying?" He rounded on her, so tall that for the first time in her life she felt dwarfed.

"Why, nothing." She was determined not to let him rattle her.

An experienced traveller she had laid out what she would be wearing the next day before collapsing into the hotel's very comfortable bed. White silk-cotton top with an oval neck, and long sleeves she had pushed up in a concession to the heat. White linen trousers—lovely flattering cut—and white-and-tan loafers. Borrowing a bit of Bella's dash she added a studded tan leather belt to break up the all-white.

He was wearing an outfit only a notch up from yesterday. A torso-hugging black T-shirt with a white logo—I Love NY, of all things, the *love* represented by a red heart. She supposed he had been to New York many times. Brought the T-shirt back from a recent trip. Black tight-fitting jeans. He looked about as fit as a man could possibly get. Fit and disgracefully sexy. And goodness, the way he *moved*! She was right about the big jungle cat, she thought, swallowing on a slight obstruction in her throat.

"Don't be so nervous," he bid her, almost kindly, when they were seated. "I'm sure you're fully expecting a giant Territory T-bone steak, sausages, fried eggs, fried tomatoes and a pile of hash browns?"

"I'm sure it's a breakfast *you* frequently indulge in?" she countered sweetly. But how could he with that body? Next thought: as a cattle baron he would most probably work the calories off.

"You can hold the hash browns," he said, with a twist of a smile. "Though I doubt very much if you could put such a breakfast together."

Such a sensuous mouth! The four women at the table to the right of them couldn't tear their eyes off him. "What do you know of me *really*, Mr McAlpine?" She concentrated her attention away from him.

"Hardly a thing," he conceded. "Why don't we get matters out in the open? I didn't want you here, Ms Balfour, any more than *you* want to be here. But you can't escape. Neither can I. Both of us are doing this for your father. I want to keep him on board and you want to redeem yourself as I hear it?"

"Redeem myself?" Her blue eyes glinted. "Spoken by a man who listens to gossip. I'm not here to *redeem* myself—"

"Take it up with your father," he briskly interrupted, turning his arrogant head as a bestarched young waitress approached, wheeling a trolley.

"Good morning, Mr McAlpine," the waitress trilled.

"Good morning, Kym." That careless, megawatt smile. "What have you got for us there?"

He had a darn good voice too. Deep and dark, slightly grainy like polished teak, rather thrillingly vibrant, if one responded to that sort of thing.

"Just what you ordered, sir." Pretty dimples flickered in the waitress's cheek.

"No surprises, then," Olivia remarked, utilising her caustic tone.

Only then did the waitress turn her big brown eyes on Olivia. "Hope you enjoy it, ma'am."

Ma'am? Olvia allowed no one to see her reaction. She might have been taken for his maiden aunt. Cheek of the girl!

The waitress began setting out freshly squeezed fruit juice in frosted glasses—grapefruit for both—slices of a lush-looking papaya with quartered limes, leaving the remaining boiled eggs and piping hot toast under cover on the trolley. Tea or coffee would be served at the table. McAlpine had only to raise a lazy finger.

"Nice to see you again, Mr McAlpine," the young woman gushed by way of farewell, injecting all she had in the way of oomph. As it happened, rather a lot.

"Another admirer?" Olivia enquired, after the waitress had gone, allowing the scoff to show.

"Do you mind, Ms Balfour?" He picked up his glass of fruit juice, toasted her with it. "Hope everything is to your satisfaction?"

"Thank you, yes," Olivia admitted, deciding to be gracious.

"So eat up because we're outta here!" His dynamic features tightened. Abruptly he had sprung into tycoon mode right before her eyes. Not that she hadn't seen it all before. But had her father seriously considered in sending her to Clint McAlpine he had sent her in fathoms deep. Not that she wasn't an excellent swimmer. She had come to Australia determined on setting her mind to the task and in so doing reaffirming her self-worth. It would hardly do to give up at the outset.

Onward Christian soldiers.

At school they had used to sing that in chapel. And, oh, yes. "Amazing Grace."

Even so it would be a titanic effort.

He came to her room just as she was wondering what to do with all her luggage. In retrospect she had brought rather a lot. Probably what she really needed was some khaki bush clothes, a slouch hat and stout boots to ward off possible snake attacks. She had read all about the snakes, the dingoes, the wild buffalo and the wild pigs, not to mention the crocodiles. Maybe she should tell him she had some experience of the African bush, though the place she and Bella had stayed at—the owner was the father of one of Bella's admirers—was extremely comfortable. No magnificent wild animals were shot when they had been taken out on safari. She couldn't have tolerated that. But she and Bella had adored the sightseeing.

Now the Northern Territory, the Top End. *Terra incognito!*

She swung her head at the peremptory tap on the door, shocked that she felt nervous of the man.

"Do you usually travel so light?" he asked, his gleaming eyes on the pile-up of Louis Vuitton.

"Only when I'm on safari."

"No chance, then, of seeing you naked?"

She reacted, if she thought of it, like an outraged virgin. "I beg your pardon!"

"Please, a joke, Ms Balfour." He groaned, casting an eye on her luggage once more. "Might be an idea if you tried to lighten up a little. You're not at home now. Bring a couple of the smaller pieces. What you most need. I'll get someone to collect the rest and fly it back to the station."

Olivia lifted a delicate shoulder. He was making her feel rather foolish. Pompous to boot. "As you wish."

"Forget the safari—you couldn't have brought more if you were boarding the *QE2* for a trans-Atlantic trip."

"I've brought nothing out of the ordinary, I assure you." She turned away, to save face, picking out two pieces of luggage and her small make-up box. She had brought lashings of sunblock.

"Right, now we can get under way." He hoisted her two pieces of luggage—quite heavy, in fact—and tucked one under his arm, carrying the other as easily as if it were a cardboard box. "I have a city apartment," he told her in an offhand manner. "We'll take a cab there."

She reacted with a frown. "What for?"

He gave her a brief, impatient glance. "Certainly not wild sex, if you had that in mind. There's a helipad on the roof. The complex was built by one of the McAlpine companies. We're going by helicopter."

"Oh!" She gave a nonchalant wave of the hand to cover immense flurry. Wild sex? *Lead me not into temptation.* "That's OK. I've travelled by helicopter before. My father owns an island retreat in the Caribbean."

"Squillions could only dream of owning one!" he cried satirically. "Good, then you won't be nervous. Your father is a very rich man."

"I believe you are so regarded."

Unexpectedly he gave her one of his slashing smiles. "How quaint! So regarded! But should that worry me?"

She abruptly exploded. He was looking at her as though she was stuck in a time warp. "I have no idea what you mean."

"Money is a powerful aphrodisiac," he pointed out.

As though *she* needed to be told that. "You'll be pleased to know I have absolutely no interest in you, Mr McAlpine, romantic or otherwise." So why was she feeling decidedly *hot.* There was the possibility if he so much as touched her she could go up in flames.

"For the record, that makes two of us, Ms Balfour. Anyway, no offence, but you're a little too buttoned up for me."

She didn't deign to reply. On the other hand she was unexpectedly dismayed. Buttoned up, was she? In her view she had always been so well behaved that she should have been given a medal. The lift arrived, unloading two smiling guests and a porter with a luggage trolley.

"I'll take those Mr McAlpine," the porter said. "You're going to the helipad?"

"Yes, thank you, Arnold," McAlpine said with a smile.

"Beautiful day for flying."

"Perfect!"

"Good gracious!" Olivia burst out in surprise as she looked towards the waiting helicopter where a group of men were standing.

"You can't back out now, Ms Balfour," McAlpine told her with a mocking sideways glance.

"I didn't mean that at all. I'm actually looking forward to the flight. It's the helicopter. I've never seen one like it before."

"Goodness, and I thought you'd seen everything. Maybe not *done* everything."

"And what is that supposed to mean?" Her tone, had she known it, was cool on the way to arctic. Victorian, really.

"A fairly harmless remark, I would have thought. What you're looking at—what we'll be flying in—is the newest addition to McAlpine Aviation which has a three-state charter. The Territory, Western Australia and Queensland. You may not know—then again you might, as I suspect you're a very well-read woman—Qantas, the national carrier, spells out *Queensland and Northern Territory Aerial Services*. It was founded in 1920 and it's actually the oldest continuously operating airline in the English-speaking world."

"I did fly Qantas from Singapore," she said, finding herself caught up in the story.

"At the time of our worst cyclone ever—Cyclone Tracy which

devastated Darwin—Qantas established a world record when six hundred and seventy-three people were evacuated on a single Boeing 747. I was just three at the time but I vividly remember it."

"The cyclone or the flight?" She shaded her eyes to look up at him. It was surprisingly good to have to look up at a man. Even if it was McAlpine.

"Both. My family has always had a keen interest in aviation. My grandfather, Roscoe McAlpine, established McAlpine Aviation. General air charter, jet charter, helicopter, freight. Supporting government agencies with fire and flood operations. That kind of thing. We've grown exponentially since Granddad's day. He would have been so proud. The irony is he was killed in a light aircraft crash when he was a very experienced pilot who had flown hundreds of hours in very hazardous conditions." He shrugged fatalistically, but Olivia could see the hidden grief.

"Am I the only passenger?" she asked, looking uncertainly towards the waiting men.

"Do you need reassurance? They're not cattle rustlers. All three are company employees. They're coming with us," he supplied briefly.

And pray tell exactly where?

She had the sense not to ask.

Words simply could not describe her feelings as Olivia looked down at the primeval wilderness that was to be her home for the next five months. It would be fair to say she was shocked out of her mind.

Dear God! she prayed fervently. *How am I going to be able to withstand it?*

God answered very promptly. *Buck up!*

The famous early explorers of this continent—splendid, intrepid men of British stock—would have quailed at the prospect of having to transverse such a place, which looked to her distraught eyes like no other kind on earth. What lay beneath her had to be one of the last remaining great wilderness areas on the planet.

There was no sign of human intervention, let alone habitation, apart from the lonely cluster of white buildings that looked like an outback version of Stonehenge. Extraordinary as it may appear, she couldn't think she would enjoy her stay at all. This vast landscape glowed as fiery as Mars, the red soil held together by what looked like giant pincushions in the most amazing shades of burnt gold and burnt orange. And she with the English-rose complexion! She would probably shrivel up in a matter of days.

Don't allow yourself to get fazed.

She knew it was extremely important to maintain order of the mind. Order, after all, was the bedrock of her being. She was a Balfour and a Capricorn to boot.

The two men McAlpine had taken on board were fortyish, lean outback characters in cowboy regalia. Both looked as if they could easily wrestle a bullock to the ground, but they were most courteous and soft spoken when introduced. They sat up close to McAlpine, the boss, often exchanging remarks in unison. The "great minds think alike" syndrome, she thought.

She had been allotted a seat in the farthest row, deciding there and then she wouldn't let McAlpine see how the sight of his ancestral home was affecting her. She realised everyone couldn't live in a stately home but this rather beggared belief.

She wouldn't have need of any of the nice things she had brought with her. They would be as out of place in these surroundings as one of Bella's outlandish sequinned party dresses.

Bella, oh, Bella, what did we do? She hoped her twin—she was missing her dreadfully—didn't feel as scared as she did.

What are you scared of? McAlpine?

Minutes later they landed, smooth as a bird, on the front lawn of the homestead, a green oasis in the fiery red wilderness that went on and on and on, so it seemed to fill the known world. Towering palms, graceful unfamiliar trees and a riot of prodigally blossoming shrubs offered all-round protection to the building which looked hardly bigger than a cottage. She could see a silver stream snaking away into the distance. She wondered if crocodiles, flourishing as a protected species, sunned themselves on the banks, using them for slipways.

Safely on the ground now, she looked around her with stoicism. Eventually it came to her.

He's having me on!

Well, she could take a joke as well as the next woman. Even with her sunglasses on she had to shade her eyes from the fierce, glittering sun. She tried to focus on the homestead and its square white facade. It was a genuinely *small* timber construction set on very high concrete piers, probably for ventilation and to keep the building above possible flooding. Latticework closed the space in, acting as a trellis for a magnificent flowering vine with huge bell-like golden-yellow flowers. And such a fragrance! One could get drunk on it.

The roof of the homestead was corrugated iron painted green, as were the shutters on the French doors that opened out onto the broad covered veranda. Planter-style chairs were set at intervals along with huge pots of rather wonderful tropical plants. More astonishing plants with great curling fernlike waves grew profusely out of hanging baskets. Hot or not, with a little TLC and a drop of precious water one could maintain a dream of an indoor garden. A vision of Balfour Manor's splendid English gardens—especially the rose gardens—broke before her eyes.

Home! Oh, God! More than ever she felt like a fish out of water.

On the thick springy grass, she soon discovered she was wobbly on her feet. "OK?" McAlpine broke away from his men to take her by the arm with what seemed genuine concern.

"I'm perfectly *fine,* thank you," she said stiffly, somewhat intimidated by the vibrant male sexuality.

"That's strange. I could have sworn you were thinking, *Where the hell am I?*"

"Then never distrust your intuitions, Mr McAlpine," she returned coolly. "Where exactly *are* we?" Two could play at a joke.

"You're on Naroo Waters."

"And it's *charming*." She gave him a bright social smile, clearly feigned.

"I'm very fond of it too." His eyes glittered pure gold as he looked at her. "I've visited it over and over since I was a boy. This is one of our outstations, Ms Balfour, as I'm sure you've guessed. I've stopped to offload Wes and Bernie and a few supplies. Wes manages the place. Bernie is his leading hand."

"You weren't willing to tell me before?" she asked sweetly.

"I operate on a need–to-know basis, Ms Balfour."

"While *I* think you were testing me out."

He laughed. Far too attractive a sound. "OK, you passed. Totally unexpected, I have to say. Now, while I have a talk to Wes, you might like to go into the house. Heather will make you a cup of tea. Heather is his wife. I'll be along presently."

"And who shall I say I am?" she asked haughtily. He did bring out the worst in her.

"Let's pretend you're a friend," he said and walked away.

As she approached the homestead a small woman with a mop of orange curls wearing a green tank top and cream shorts to the knee ran out onto the veranda to wave.

"You must be Olivia," she called in such a way Olivia felt a most welcome visitor, not a total stranger who had just landed very noisily on the lawn. "Please come in." Again not in the polite meaningless way Olivia had often been guilty of in the past, but as though she really meant it. "I've got a nice cup of tea for you and a slice of my raisin cake. Just baked it."

The cake was excellent, with a delicious walnut crunch. The tea was just the way she liked it. Added to that the sheer niceness of Heather Finlay—a good Scottish name—and it all went a long way towards calming Olivia's nerves.

They sat in the homestead's small living room which was as comfortable and attractive as anyone could make the postage-stamp space. Large white ceiling fans whirred overhead. The furnishings were cane, the two sofas and the armchairs upholstered in emerald-green cotton patterned in white, maintaining the tropical look. The feature wall held four huge blown-up photographs of different tropical flowers set in a frame. It was cost effective as well as striking.

Close to Heather, Olivia could see that she was older than she first appeared. At a guess early forties, with a trim figure, a redhead's freckled skin and green eyes with dancing lights.

"I take it you're on holiday?" Heather's eyes lingered on Olivia as though she were a creature from a fairy tale with fairy-tale clouds of golden blonde hair.

Olivia decided to tell the truth. Shame the devil. She almost—not quite—believed in him. "I'm here to help out Mr McAlpine in any way I can, Heather. A business arrangement, really. My father is a shareholder in the McAlpine Pastoral Company. I'm very interested in learning as much as I can about it and of course being helpful while I'm at it."

Heather's face lit up with what looked like a triumphant smile.

Why was that?

"You'll be *perfect* to help with the big end-of-the-year functions Clint hosts," Heather supplied the answer. "I suppose Clint had that in mind. You'll have met Marigole, his ex-wife?"

"Actually, no!" *Marigole? Ah, the unusual name.* Olivia set down her pretty teacup. Royal Doulton's Regalia. She suspected Heather had used her best, which was nice. "I don't know Mr McAlpine all that well. We've met at a couple of functions in London and once at a wedding we both attended in Scotland. There's some family connection between the Balfours and the McAlpines from way back. But his wife—his ex-wife, I should say—wasn't with him at the time."

Heather gave an eye roll. "Well, I suppose it's getting pretty close on two years ago the divorce came through." Heather poured them a second cup of tea. "Good Scottish names. Balfour and McAlpine. Balfour means *pasture land*, doesn't it?"

"You're very well informed, Heather." Olivia was taken by surprise.

"Scottish background me ain self." Heather laid on an accent. "Same as Wes. I daresay your family retain a good many pastures?" She flashed a teasing smile.

"Nothing on par with *this*, Heather! I wasn't prepared for *this*!"

"You sound like you're a wee bit scared of the place?"

"I'd like to say no, but actually it is daunting," Olivia confessed. "The vastness, the isolation, the lack of human habitation and the floods of light! Nature is supreme here."

"That it is," Heather agreed.

"You must get lonely from time to time?" Olivia asked, even though she could see Heather was a strong spirit.

"Sometimes I do!" Heather freely admitted. "Especially since we sent our boys off to boarding school. That's a couple of years back. They're twelve. Twins! They'll be home soon for the June vacation. If it gets a bit much for me or if Wes is away on a long muster, I take a trip into Darwin. I've got friends there."

"So you'll be looking forward to having your sons home." Olivia didn't doubt it.

"Alex and Ewan." Heather's green eyes lit up. "I adore them."

"I'm a twin," Olivia confided, feeling an instant of crushing loneliness for Bella and home. "My sister's name is Bella. She's very beautiful."

"Well, she would be." Heather laughed, still looking at Olivia with unfeigned admiration. "Like you."

"Goodness, no!" Olivia shook her head. "We're fraternal twins, not identical. Bella takes after our mother. She was a recognised beauty. We lost our mother when we were toddlers."

"Now that's sad!" Heather's expression sobered.

"One is shaped by it, I always think. At any rate one develops very finely tuned emotional antennae."

"But you have your dad?" Heather was regarding her visitor keenly.

"Not as much as we would have liked," Olivia found herself revealing. Her *inner* person as opposed to her *outer* person appeared to be emerging at a rate of knots. "My father is an important man and a workaholic."

"Well, it does go with the territory, love," Heather said consolingly. "I'm sure he's very proud of you and Bella."

Olivia further surprised herself. "Well, we *hope* to make him proud, Heather. We live to please him because we love him."

Heather made a little face. "I can see I'm talking to a very modest young woman."

They had slipped into conversation so easily it was obvious Heather was starved of female company and ready for a chat, if not a good gossip. What struck Olivia as out of the ordinary was that Heather appeared to have taken to her on sight, when she knew scores of people who called her standoffish and a lot worse behind her back. It would have shocked them to know how shy she really was when the layers of cool polished veneer were stripped off. The trouble was, as the years went by she got better and better at playing cool. But it was all a facade. All the people who loved her knew that.

So apparently did Heather. And Bessie, her Good Samaritan. She hoped to see Bessie again.

Heather spoke gently. "You'll be a good mother when the time comes. I take it you're not married?" She had taken note of Olivia's elegant ringless hands.

Olivia sighed. "It would be fantastic to meet the right man."

"But you must have heaps of admirers." Heather wasn't trying to flatter. She thought her visitor very beautiful and refined. Also, her upper-class English voice fell entrancingly on the ear. Heather was impressed.

"Bella is the one with the admirers." Olivia's smile held pride and affection. "She's very quirky. Funny as well as being stunningly beautiful. I missed out on the quirkiness. I tend to keep a much lower profile. Bella is very much at ease with herself. I'm a bit on the bland side, I'm afraid."

"Nothing wrong with that," said Heather, thinking her visitor anything but bland. Obviously the sister had a strong sense of her own beauty, whereas Olivia, for some unfathomable reason, did not. "Anyway, outback life instead of big-city life is guaranteed to bring anyone out of their shell. I know you're going to love Kalla Koori. It's one of the outback's great showplaces."

Of course it was, as befitting outback royalty.

"I'm looking forward to staying there."

Heather leaned forward confidentially. "Just between you, me and the gatepost, which incidentally is a good few miles away, I should tell you Marigole still likes to pop in from time to time. *Unannounced.* As you don't know her and you'll be staying on the station, I feel a little word of warning mightn't go astray. Marigole is very territorial, divorced or not. We're all convinced she wants him back."

"Really?" It wasn't the discreet thing to do but Olivia decided to follow up Heather's lead. Listening carefully, one always learned something interesting, or potentially useful. Just think of the journalist who had spilt the beans on her family. "How did they come to split up in the first place?" She knew her questioning Heather wasn't the done thing but she really wanted to know. McAlpine wasn't about to tell her a thing.

Heather leaned in. "Marigole put it about she was totally fed up with the lifestyle, the fact Clint was never there for her when goodness knows he has a *huge* job on his hands, but it was the other way around, I be thinking. You know they have a daughter?"

Olivia nodded and waited for Heather to continue.

"Georgina. Used to be a little honey but the divorce upset her terribly plus puberty hit her hard, as they say. Marigole pretty well abandoned her when this new guy came along. Lucas something, a merchant banker. Last year Clint's aunt Buffy acted as his hostess and did a marvellous job of it but sadly her health has declined of recent times. It was a terrible grief and shock to her—to us all—when Mr McAlpine was killed. Lady Venetia—that's Buffy—lost her brother and Clint lost his father."

Olivia of the tender heart bowed her head. She had learned from her own father that Kyle McAlpine had been killed in a freak accident on a mining site. Clint McAlpine's mother lived in Melbourne; one sister, Alison, had married a wealthy American business man and lived in New York. The other sister, Catriona, was a lawyer in London. Something to do with international law. She thought she had that right.

"Remember that character Joan Collins used to play on *Dynasty*?" Heather asked.

"I know of Joan Collins, of course. A beautiful ageless woman, but the series was before my time."

"You should catch the reruns," Heather advised. "Joan played a marvellous bitch, Alexis, the divorced wife, but I have to tell you, Marigole could give *her* lessons."

Confidences were abruptly cut short.

"Hell, it's Clint!" Heather turned in her chair so her eye was on the front door. "Not a word of this to him, love."

"Goodness, no!" Olivia was aghast. "Mum's the word."

"It's really not like me to gossip, especially not about the boss, but I spotted you for an innocent right off." Heather hastily demolished what was left of her raisin cake. "In my experience—and I used to be a nurse for the Flying Doctors Service—a timely warning never goes astray." She spoke as though her confidences were strategic manoeuvres Olivia should have at the ready. "As soon as Marigole hears you're on Kalla Koori, she'll descend like a bat out of hell."

Olivia, blessed and sometimes cursed with a highly visual imagination, half covered her face. She had visions of a Caribbean fruit bat sinking its teeth into her like a ripe mango.

CHAPTER THREE

From the air she looked down on a great many deep pools of water that glittered an unearthly blue-green. Crocodile lagoons, she wondered with a shudder. Prehistoric monsters existing in such beauty. In the distance to either side were more pools of emerald green and a long winding river that cut through fiery low ridges and endless giant fingers of sand dunes.

A jagged cliff with sheer rock walls that glowed a range of dry ochres—pinks, reds, yellows, creams and blacks, with deep purple slashed into the narrow ravines—served as the most dramatic backdrop possible for Kalla Koori's massive homestead. She had been expecting colonial architecture and the quintessential verandas. This was something completely different. More in keeping with a desert environment with a touch of Morocco. The house from the air had an endless expanse of roof line with a central two- maybe three-storey tower. It stood in the very centre of what looked like a fortified desert village.

Here at last was the McAlpine stronghold.

Presumably in times of torrential cyclones McAlpine could offer shelter to the entire population of Darwin beneath the homestead roof, Olivia thought, her breath taken by the spectacle beneath her. The base of the stand-alone cliff appeared to be in permanent shadow. It was marked by a border of lush green where water must gather and never entirely dry out. All else was a million square miles of uninhabited desert—a beautiful, savage place unlike anything she had ever seen. She could well imagine the most superbly engineered four-wheel drives sinking into the bottomless red shifting sands, never to be seen again. There was a great deal to be feared about this environment.

But goodness! One could well find passion and romance here.

Astounded by her flight of fancy, she endeavoured to get a grip even though her pulses were jumping wildly. It had to be one of her increasingly mad moments, or alternatively it could be taken as an indicator she had at long last become aware life was shooting by like a falling star. That's what came of having to play the archetypal earth mother to her siblings. She was starting to imagine herself as a woman standing at the edge of a cliff like the one that towered beneath them. Either she could totter for ever as she had done all her life or take a spectacular dive. Truth be told, she was sick to death of being *sensible*. Bella was *never* sensible. Indeed a lot of her escapades had been hare-brained, but at least Bella had fun.

McAlpine landed the helicopter to the right of a giant hangar at least a mile away from the home compound. The interior looked as though it could well hold a fleet of Airbuses. The station insignia—Kalla Koori—was emblazoned in chrome yellow and cobalt blue on the roof. The Australian flag that stood on a tall pole nearby only moments before hanging limp suddenly whipped to attention, unfurling its length. Probably as much honouring McAlpine's arrival as the buffeting from the chopper's rotors, Olivia thought a touch sharply.

They were met by a tall bearded man in a check shirt and jeans, a huge white Akubra tilted back on his head. "Boss!" he said, straightening up. He had been leaning nonchalantly against a four-wheel drive, its metallic Duco throwing off iridescent lights. Again, the station insignia in blue and gold was on the door panel.

"Norm." Briefly McAlpine introduced them. This was Norman Cartwright, who with his wife, Kath, ran the domestic affairs of the station—Kath with her team in the house, Norm with his team in the extensive compound grounds. She liked Norm on sight. She expected the same would go for his wife. Australians with the exception of McAlpine were warm and friendly. She bore in mind she was yet to meet the terrifying ex-wife, Marigole. Not that she hadn't met her fair share of enormously pretentious women dripping hauteur. It was unsettling to remind herself McAlpine had called her an ice princess. She wasn't an ice princess at all; she had simply perfected faking it.

McAlpine handed her into the back seat of a Range Rover, big cat eyes glistening, while he sat up front with his man, asking him a series of questions for which Norm very wisely had the answers. From long experience with her father she knew employees had all necessary information to hand or they were out the door.

Splendidly wrought iron gates hung on immense stone piers. They opened inwards as they approached, forming an impressive doorway in the ten-foot-high walls washed in a bright yellow-ochre that mirrored elements in the landscape. These walls surrounded the compound in a most protective manner; not from human invasion mercifully but the power of the elements. The massive height and the vivid desert colour put her in mind of Luis Barragán, the great Mexican architect and garden designer. An extraordinarily beautiful pink-tangerine bougainvillea of great arching sprays and green trailing vines all but covered them. She had never seen that exact colour in a bougainvillea before.

Inside the courtyard was paradise in isolation. Something right out of an Arabian romance.

Olivia looked about her in fascination. As her father's daughter, she had been surrounded by all the trappings of wealth and power from birth, but she was quickly learning there were all kinds of excellence in architectural design. What confronted her was a far cry from Balfour Manor and its beautiful cool temperate English gardens. Balfour's garden design had, in fact, been widely copied in Europe. Here the sun reigned supreme, just as it did in Arabia, the Middle East, Mexico, South America. What spread before her had a look of a garden the Arab world might have developed from unsurpassed Persian models.

Water rippled from a great stone central fountain and splashed over the edges of several large basins into a very long but relatively narrow water-lily-strewn pond almost large enough to be called a canal. A broad circular drive led to the desert mansion, allowing for multiple parking. The big house itself washed in a darker ochre than the walls, and could easily be taken for the Moroccan pavilion. A series of colonnaded arches, with beautiful coloured tiles wrapped around the columns, framed a two-storey central portico with the traditional arch that led to the front door.

Given such a large space to work with the designer had offset the broad drive with a series of irrigation channels, or rills, which formed a grid of sparkling water. The grid ran back and forth across much of the length and breadth of the great courtyard. She was aware the grid she was looking at was developed from an ancient tradition. The very sight and sound of the rippling waters was sufficient to cool the atmosphere.

Truly magnificent date palms had been perfectly placed, their enormous shooting heads in themselves resembled fountains. Looking up at them she recalled what the prophet Mahomet was said to have told his followers: *Honour the date palm for it is your mother.* In the desert fringes of the world that ran across North Africa through the Middle East to Pakistan, the date palm was life. It signalled oases and water beneath the sand, provided food, wine, sugar, oil, shelter, even stock fodder. The date palm obviously thrived in the great desert areas of Australia.

McAlpine broke into her train of thought, his voice as seductive as dark molasses. "I do hope everything is to your liking, Ms Balfour?"

She unbent sufficiently to show her pleasure. "This is a magical place." She had to push away the thought he possessed more than a dash of magic himself, with his boundless self-confidence, and acute awareness as though he was reading her mind.

"High praise for a woman not easily pleased!" he said very drily. "When we landed on Naroo you kept throwing glances my way, suggesting I might at some stage be tempted to throw you to the crocodiles."

"What nonsense!" She thought she had hidden her panic rather well.

"Well, don't get *too* complacent," he warned, observing the way her classic blonde head was perched so elegantly on her long swan's neck. "We do have plenty of crocs on Kalla Koori, but I won't introduce you to them until you're ready. Now shall we go inside? You must find it hot standing the sun."

"Oddly enough I'm getting used to it. That or the fountain and the running water are creating a wonderful illusion of coolness. The design, the massive walls and the vivid colours bring Moroccan architecture to mind. Then maybe the Mexican architect—"

"Luis Barragán?"

"Yes."

"I'm sure you've visited Marrakesh, but have you ever been to Mexico?" It surprised him the odd unexpected pleasure she gave him. At their last meeting he'd as good as told her she was a genuine pain in the neck. She was in a way, but he realised even then he had wanted to know *more*. What lay behind the arctic mask, for instance? Except back then he was a married man on the verge of divorce.

"Not as yet," she was saying in her lovely voice. A saving grace even when it was caustic. "But I'd love to go. I know the Caribbean where Daddy has his island. I've visited Cuba, stayed at a friend's villa in Havana. But I do know the architect's work. He won the equivalent of the Nobel prize for architecture?" She looked up at him for confirmation, surprising him studying her as intently as a scientist might study a rare butterfly.

McAlpine shifted his gaze. Even in strong sunlight she had the most beautiful flawless skin. "The Pritzker Prize. My parents and I were allowed to see his house and garden and one other, Casa Antonio Gálvez. Barragán treated the house and garden as one. My mother, in particular, fell madly in love with the soaring walls, the stunning colours and the marvellous sense of intimacy within the houses. She never did like huge plate-glass windows—'glass boxes' she called them. Inappropriate for here anyway," he said. "We have all the nature we need right outside the compound gates. We don't need it inside the house. My mother thought the vivid blocks of colour would be perfect for Kalla Koori. Colours that could stand up to the brilliant sunlight. When you think about it, Barrigán's colours are echoed in the striations of the sandstone cliff up there."

"So they are!" She pressed her hands together in silent applause. "The cliff is a wonderful landmark. It adds enormously to the atmosphere. Spiritual, I feel. Tell me, when was the homestead built?"

He took a moment to answer. "My parents started it," he answered rather sombrely. "I finished it. My mother finds it too painful to visit often but she does come. The original homestead took a battering with Cyclone Tracy. What we have here has been built to withstand another cyclone of that magnitude."

"And it's splendid! I can't wait to see inside."

"Well, why don't we do that now," he invited smoothly. "You can't imagine how happy you've made me."

The mocking golden gaze stabbed her through. "Do *not* try to patronise me, Mr McAlpine, thank you very kindly." She had the fearful notion he was hypnotising her, because everything else was being shut out.

"I'm not trying to patronise you, Ms Balfour," he assured her suavely. "How could I when you yourself have developed it to an art form. I'm merely trying to colonise you on the run as it were. Turn you into an impromptu Aussie."

"It might take longer than five months." Her tone was back to lofty.

"Oh, my heaven!" Brackets offset the generous, sexy mouth. "I'd all but forgotten you were going to be with us for such a short time. What a pity! You might have blotted your copybook first up but I have to say you're perking up." They were moving beneath the tall double-storey portico lined with magnificent clumping palms with slender stems and pinnate-leaf plants in huge terracotta pots. "You ride?"

Near outraged by such a question Olivia lowered her head

from inspecting the inlaid domed ceiling. "What do you mean!" she asked shortly. "Of course I ride."

"I mean *seriously*?" He was teasing her. Couldn't help it. She was incredibly starchy.

"Only something very, very *quiet*," she returned sarcastically. "Oh, come on! Like you, I was practically born in the saddle. I know you're only trying to take a rise out of me. Just like the other times we've met."

"You remember, do you?"

His smile twisted her heart. In fact, the man was starting to make her feel as if she had been hibernating in a nunnery all her life.

Being a Balfour she was able to respond coolly. "I didn't know if you hated women or it was just me."

"More my ex-wife," he supplied very bluntly. "She was making life very difficult at the time. If I made you unhappy, if only for a few seconds, I apologise."

"Not to worry." Olivia waved a hand, though she was experiencing an unfamiliar sensation of heat through her blood. "A few seconds can seem rather a lot."

"And you don't take kindly to any form of criticism?"

"It was rather *more* than that as I recall." She needed a cold drink to quench the heat. It was coming from inside, not from out.

"Oddly enough I did like you." He took her arm, moving with languid near-animal grace. "So what was Oscar thinking about sending you to me?"

She spoke tartly. "All I can say is he likes the *weirdest* people."

"And that's how you see me?" He burst out laughing—a genuine laugh, not in the least put out.

"No, not weird precisely. I do apologise. But you were *provoking* me which was rather terrible because I thought I did nothing to warrant it."

"Maybe you need time to take a good hard look at yourself?" he suggested.

"Might I remind you of the same thing?" She looked pointedly away, taking the opportunity to study her surroundings. It was all so very, very unexpected. "This really is the most fascinating place. Its fascination is increased ten times over by the extraordinary location. I should tell you I haven't the faintest idea what you require of me." She brought her blue eyes back to him "You seem to have confirmed my strong suspicion to see me grounded."

"As opposed to looking down from your lofty pedestal?" His tone was challenging.

"I don't know why you had that silly idea. It's talk. Just *talk*. I'm really a very down-to-earth person."

A scoffing sound came from deep in his throat. "What you *definitely* aren't is down-to-earth, Ms Balfour. And why would you be? You've lived a life of enormous wealth and privilege. You wouldn't have the slightest idea how ordinary people live."

"And I suppose *you* would?" she retorted, stung. She knew her blood pressure was soaring.

"Ms Balfour, the only way we're going to survive the next five months is to try to be tolerant of each other."

"And that's your idea of tolerant, is it?" She had to shield her eyes from him. The man was so dazzling, he was dangerous.

"Well, you must concede I've had to work very hard to measure up to what my father expected of me. Harder still to take over from him. You, on the other hand, unless I'm mistaken, have been solely occupied opening a fete or two and drinking endless cups of tea."

The blue blaze in her eyes spoke volumes. "I'd go much further than that. I've worked hard on my charities. As well, I've acted on any number of occasions as hostess for my father," she pointed out icily. "No easy job either."

"So there we have it, a starting place. As it happens I'll be needing an experienced hostess to organise and run several functions I'll be holding over the coming months. You could very well be roped in to that. Also—surprise, surprise—you might have to run the house for a while. Piece of cake after the manor.

I'm planning on sending Norm and Kath off on a well-earned vacation. Don't panic." He held up a staying hand as she went to voice a protest. "That's if they want to go."

With an effort she calmed her rapid breathing. "You mean you expect me to take over as housekeeper?"

"Remind yourself you seek the common touch. No need to be outraged. Besides, you're here to work for me, in any capacity I choose. I haven't gone overboard and asked you to pretend you're my English fiancée. Though that would solve a few problems. Possibly create a whole lot more. Anyway, you work for me. That was the deal. We have plenty of staff. I scarcely expect you to do the vacuuming, but I haven't the slightest doubt you're an excellent organiser."

"I told you not to patronise me." She gritted her white teeth.

"Need I patronise you? Oh, there's another thing. You know I have a daughter?"

"I do. Georgina. I thought you might have told me long before this."

"I'm telling you now. Georgy is beautiful. She resembles her mother. In looks. She's my favourite person in the whole world. I love her dearly. But I have to warn you—she'll be here a week on Saturday—that she's going through a most difficult stage. But then you'd be used to that with all your sisters?"

All her sisters? Well, she did have rather a lot. "Do you want me to tick them off one by one?" she asked acidly.

"Not necessary. It's just reassuring to me to know you've had all that experience playing the cool, competent, sensible big sister."

"So you're asking me—*telling* me—I'll be your difficult young daughter's babysitter while she's here? She could well dislike and resent me."

"What's to dislike?" His mouth quirked. "I'm hoping you'll be her friend. She's had a lot of trouble accepting the divorce. She used to be a straight-A student but her grades have slipped of recent times. She'll be staying on for a good month or so."

Olivia frowned. "Given that her grades are falling why is she's being allowed to have so much time away from school?"

His expression turned serious. "She hasn't been all that well. Not eating. That kind of thing. The school counsellor thinks she would benefit from a prolonged stay. A study program has been arranged so don't worry about that. The thing is, she's missing me. She needs me around."

"Why ever not?" Olivia huffed. "But then you would be an extremely busy man."

His gaze narrowed. "One can easily see you've had big issues with your own father, Ms Balfour. Might I be allowed to put in a word for him? Oscar would have had to spend a great deal of his time rebuilding and greatly expanding the Balfour business empire. You may have felt neglected but I'm sure you realise you and your many sisters have reaped the reward."

She swallowed hard at his tone. Obviously a reprimand. "Of course we do."

"It's not easy being the man at the top. Anyway, my ex-wife, Marigole, and her current partner will be bringing Georgy here to me. To make things easier all-round I've invited a few house guests to act as a buffer. They'll be arriving on the Saturday morning and leaving Sunday afternoon. We'll have a small dinner party, ten of us in all. Georgy won't be attending. Too young.'

"And your housekeeper knows all about it?" Olivia queried. "I would think she's superefficient?"

"Indeed she is," he agreed, "but I'm sure she'd be delighted if you could impart some of your own splendid expertise. Menus, table settings, flowers and so forth. Kath isn't quite in your league. She doesn't need to be, of course. My mother was a wonderful hostess. So is my aunt Buffy aka Lady Venetia Massingham. But Buffy isn't up to it these days and my mother can't abide my ex-wife."

"May one wonder why?" She couldn't resist the touch of sarcasm. "You must have loved her when you married her?"

"I must have. God, it's hard to remember."

"That sounds very callous," she offered censure.

"Don't overstep the mark, Ms Balfour," he warned with cutting suavity. "I was married when I was twenty-four. Marigole had scores of admirers but for some reason she only wanted me."

"Perhaps you were more handsome and charismatic than the rest?" she suggested, making the comment as cool and clinical as she could.

"Do *you* find me handsome and charismatic?" He caught and trapped her gaze.

Major fluster. Balfour practised calm. "I've been used to handsome, charismatic men all my life, Mr McAlpine. My father is just such a man. It doesn't mean such men make good husbands and fathers."

"How harsh you are, Ms Balfour. Not surprising. I can see you're overflowing with issues."

Issues? She'd give him issues! "It may have slipped your attention, but so are you."

"I guess so," he relented. "It's just I hate to see a woman as beautiful as you so frost bound. It can't have been easy for you and your twin sister, left without a mother so very early in life?"

"We were taken excellent care of," she said repressively, giving him a sweeping blue glance.

"Of course. We'll leave that one for now. You might as well have a sign reading Do Not Disturb on your forehead."

Don't let him get to you.

"I'm a very private person," she said with something of the old hauteur.

It didn't seem to impress him. Rather the reverse. "In other words you fear to let yourself go? Let me hold out a skerrick of hope. Kalla Koori might be just the place for you to thaw out. Incidentally we can't go on addressing each other so formally."

"*You* started it," she said, realising the moment the words were out of her mouth how childish they sounded. "You set the tone."

"Then I'm unsetting it, Olivia. You may begin calling me Clint."

"As in Clint Eastwood?" she asked with mock sweetness.

"As in Clinton. Clinton was my mother's maiden name. I was baptised Reynold Clinton McAlpine. The Reynold—another family name—didn't stay around for long. It was my father who started calling me Clint. My mother had no real objection."

Fellow feeling abruptly smote her heart. "You must miss her." She could hear it in his voice. That was what made her momentarily soften her stance.

He glanced down on her briefly, his eyes so golden they warmed her skin. "I do. Both of our lives have been shadowed by my father's death. But I'm hoping that, in time, my mother will settle and come back here for long visits. Now enough confidences for today, Olivia. I need you to turn your exceptional skills initially to arranging the house party. It's not a lot of time, I know, but I'm certain a young woman of your training and background will take to it like a duck to water."

"Do I dine with your guests?" She had to remind herself she wasn't, strictly speaking, a guest.

"Good God, yes." He sounded startled. "Even though you're enormously stuck up—at least with me—I'm sure you can modify it. Anyway, with your background you'll be able to talk knowledgeably about many things of interest."

"Thank you for that," she said, sounding crisp and short. He was just so sarcastic with her! "May I ask, what about your wife? Correction, ex-wife. My presence couldn't make her very happy." That was a legitimate concern.

"What's it got to do with *her*?" His black brows drew together. Impatiently he took her arm, leading her to the magnificent double doors of brass-studded dark-stained timber that opened into the entrance hall. "You'll be acting as my PR woman. I can't see you helping with the muster or breaking in a few brumbies. You're Olivia Balfour, of the illustrious Balfour family. There's a distant connection between our families. You may like to sort that out sometime. Your father is a major shareholder in

McAlpine Enterprises. You're here on a study tour. Part work, and partly to fit in as much fun as possible. How's that?"

"Why should she believe it?"

He laughed hollowly. "Because I say so. You're not feeling intimidated by the thought of my ex-wife, are you, Olivia?"

"Hardly!" Her voice dripped hauteur. "After all, I have no romantic interest in you."

He looked down at her cool perfection. "You haven't *left* yet, Olivia," he reminded her.

She swung about swiftly; heat darkened her cheeks. "I think I can safely say it will *never* happen."

"Never say never," he mocked, his eyes never leaving her face. "For now, welcome to Kalla Koori. May your stay give you all the freedom you obviously crave."

The heartbreak of it all was, he was so *right*!

The next few days put her on her mettle. She had always had a taste for hard work. Not perhaps in the physical sense. She had never been a genuine worker as in the endless domestic chores required of most women. Not that she didn't know she was blessed. But in any case Kath Cartwright, the housekeeper, appeared to have any number of rotating staff, most of them girls who had grown up on the station and had never wanted to leave. She could hardly blame them. This was a whole new world. Even the blazing sunshine seemed to speak to her, though she took extreme care to look after her English skin.

"My gosh, aren't you beautiful!" Kath Cartwright, a good-natured, humorous woman, had remarked when McAlpine had introduced them.

That felt *good*, even if McAlpine looked somewhat sceptical

These Australians with their warmth and their frankness—McAlpine apart, of course—were encircling her soul. The three women she had so far made contact with—Bessie, Heather and Kath—all bright, cheerful women, had apparently taken to her on sight. She had to notice because it didn't happen all that often.

Bella had once told her she was a "dragon in the making." She hadn't been sparing of Bella either with her response. Much as they loved each other she and Bella were very different in temperament. Bella simply sparkled with light. Here in Australia she felt her own dormant sparkle was going up a notch or two.

It certainly made things easy for her when she and Kath got on like a house on fire. No territorial resentments from Kath that a newcomer was about to invade her kitchen and perhaps take over the running of the household if only for a short period. Kath welcomed her input as if she actually needed it when Olivia was certain she didn't. She even hung on her every word as Olivia told of her cordon bleu classes in London and Paris and her early mishaps, drawing lots of guffaws from Kath. When she was home and out on her official duties her teeth had often hurt from the number of times she'd had to clench them. Here she was being wrapped in a laid-back friendliness that required nothing of her but niceness.

No need to be on your high horse all the time, as McAlpine had so nicely phrased it.

"I can see you're used to everything grand," Kath observed, while they were enjoying morning coffee in the huge white kitchen characterised by order and function and outfitted with every conceivable modern appliance. "What about this menu for Saturday night? Let's make them sit up and take notice. Even Marigole. Her social secretary used to chase her with a lettuce leaf. We can fly in whatever you want. Plenty here, of course. A stocked pantry, freezer room. It's going to be exciting, the two of us working on this. I'll line up my best girls. I've trained them well. I'm happy to leave the dressing of the table to you." She gave Olivia a huge smile. "You look like you're superartistic."

"I hope I don't seriously disappoint you, Kath," Olivia said.

"Won't happen, love." Kath reached out with confidence to pat her hand. "I'll let you take care of the wines, as well. OK?"

"No problem. Do you know the people who will be coming?" It would be a blessing to hear a bit about them.

"Sure. You want thumbnail sketches?"

"Go for it," Olivia advised with a smile.

"There's you and Clint, of course—"

Kath said it as though she and McAlpine were already cosy. "We're not an item, Kath," Olivia hastened to explain, annoyed there was a slight waver in her voice.

"Believe me," said Kath, "He's a splendid catch. You don't have a certain someone back home? I suppose you do. A beautiful young woman like you."

That she was being acknowledged as a beauty caught her by surprise. "No one special, Kath."

"Don't you worry. He'll come along," Kath promised in a motherly fashion. 'Hey, you could even meet the man of your dreams here. Now where were we? There's the ex–Mrs Alpine— that's Marigole, as you know—and her latest, a rich guy called Lucas something. The Jamesons—Ncil and Celine, you'll like them—newly married, Pete and Barbara Corbett, ditto, and Brendan Fraser and his girlfriend of the moment, Chloe Sanderson. Brendan is a lot of fun, the perennial bachelor, and much sought after. He was Clint's best man. It could be a great weekend," Kath said, a note of real regret in her tone, "only Marigole takcs a particular delight in trying to torment Clint. I hope you'll cxcusc my spcaking out, dear, but you definitely need to know. I don't want you caught in thc linc of firc as it wcrc. Naturally Clint's friends—never hers—don't like it. Brendan once called her a she-devil after Marigole had been particularly appalling. Jealous of anyone Clint liked, you see. She wanted his sole attention right from the start."

"But he must have loved her, Kath." Olivia was trying to figure the marriage out. Of course, she knew people sometimes fell out of love as quickly as they fell in. But could Marigole be that bad? Heather hadn't taken to her. Now here was Kath warning her as well and obviously feeling the need. Whatever had McAlpine seen in her?

"Hey, he did for a while," Kath acknowledged. "Not love exactly, more the state of being in love. Infatuation. Marigole is a stunner. As dark as you're fair. Milky white skin, skinny as a rake, but a great clothes horse. Never seen in her in the same thing twice. Needless to say she made it her business to be charm itself until she fell pregnant. Didn't like that at all. And the way she treated me!" Kath cast up her hazel eyes. "Never mind the staff! They might as well have been invisible. Since the divorce when she's in the house she doesn't say one word to me. Anyone would think I was responsible for the split up. But it's poor little Georgy who has suffered the most."

"Now that I can understand." Olivia spoke from the heart. "No child would want their parents to divorce. It would be devastating. Especially at her age."

"Well, there's that, of course," Kath said, "but it wasn't the split so much. Georgy has always felt—with good reason—her mother never really wanted her. Marigole was cruel about that. Something Clint took violent exception to. Marigole made no bones about the fact it was a prized son she had wanted. Like she had to produce Clint's heir right off. It was a point of pride with her. Daughters came way down the line."

Olivia was utterly dismayed. Most women would be ecstatic to have a healthy child. Poor little girl. A good thing her own father didn't think like that. "There are eight of us. All daughters," she told Kath.

Kath, at the point of taking another sip of coffee, set her cup down with a clunk. "Eight?" Her eyebrows shot up to her hairline. "Your mother must have spent her life in maternity clothes?"

Olivia sighed. "Suffice to say my father has been married three times. My mother was his first wife. She died in childbirth with Zoe, the third sister. I'm the eldest by exactly two minutes. I have a twin, Bella."

"Upon my word! There's bound to be a story there!"

"I'll tell you sometime," Olivia promised.

Kath nodded "Whenever you're ready. Just remember, dear, I'm here if you ever feel like a chat. None of us want you to be lonely when you're so far from home."

A kind thought went a very long way. Olivia tucked that away for future reference.

CHAPTER FOUR

"How's it going?"

McAlpine strode through the front door—a lion of a man—bringing with him such a rush of male vigour and vitality it created its own excitement. His eyes, skin and thick auburn hair gleamed with health. She supposed he had the best physique of any man she had ever seen in her life. At any rate, every pulse in her body had jumped to attention. She had been calmly minding her own business, walking head bent, across the tiled entrance hall, a beautiful damask-and-lace tablecloth draped over her arm—one she had chosen from a whole pile that would have been suitable for any dinner party, anywhere. Now this! She was well aware McAlpine had to be extraordinarily intelligent to do what he did, but the good fairy at his christening had really gone overboard with the largesse.

"I'm on top of it already," she said crisply. The man always put her on her mettle.

"So I've heard." His eyes roamed over her, amused by her businesslike attitude. So far as he could see, she wore it like a defensive shield. Obviously she had decided it was the way to go, protecting herself at every level. In rebuilding his fortune Oscar Balfour would have had to work extremely hard. What his daughter Olivia had seriously needed was a whole lot of undivided attention. He wasn't being sarcastic when he had suggested she craved it. The deep reserve she manifested—the touch-me-not persona—was in his view a defence mechanism.

But the way she was getting on with Kath, Norm and the staff had come as something of a surprise. Obviously with them she had dropped her lady-of-the-manor guise. He took a moment now to give her *his* undivided attention. No difficulty there. She was something to see in informal dress—well-cut jeans combined with a simple white tank top. But she looked great! It was all in the height, the ultra-slim body, the long legs, pert butt, flat stomach. Her long elegant bones had a nice cover, unlike Marigole, who wasn't happy unless her bones were painfully on show. "You've really got Kath onside," he commended her. "I'm sure you brought your latent diplomatic skills to bear."

Don't let him take a rise out of you. Or failing that don't let him see it, Olivia's inner voice chirped up.

"Of course I haven't!" she denied calmly, resisting the natural urge to flare up. "You look pleased with yourself."

"Spot on."

He moved to join her. Olivia found herself swallowing; her throat felt so constricted and dry. Everything about the man was mesmeric. She had never met anyone remotely like him before for sheer physicality. She held the tablecloth firmly to her, uncomfortably aware there was a glitter of amusement in his eyes. Of course he thought her ridiculous, damn him!

"The sale of one of our Queensland stations has gone through," he told her.

Without looking back at him she said, "And you're happy with the price?"

"Count on it." His tone was buoyant. The big-cat gleam was in his eyes. "Your daddy will be too."

"Oddly enough my father likes you," she said in a tightly controlled tone.

"So you've said." He wagged a finger at her. "Too bad about you, my lady. What have you got there?" He glanced at what she had in her arms.

"Tablecloth for Saturday night," she returned briskly. She refused to be swept up by the power and magnetism of the man. "It's quite beautiful. There are napkins to match."

"Fine. I don't need a progress report. I have every faith in you, Olivia."

Most women would think the little brackets that framed his mouth were incredibly sexy. She opted to lower her lids. "That's good to hear."

"I've come back for something else entirely." His tone turned as brisk as hers. Probably in mockery. "You've been so on the job, I thought you might like a run around the station. You've got the layout of the house and the office. Now you get to see the great outdoors."

She couldn't for the life of her control the spurt of excitement that raced along her veins. "You don't mean to spring a crocodile on me, do you?"

A wicked smile slid across his generous mouth. "Not today. Maybe real soon. Do you know anything about guns?"

She grimaced. "I *can* shoot if that's what you mean. My father and some of his cronies like to bag pheasant in season. So many pounds a bird. That sort of thing. I don't care to join them. Not for a very long time. Guns are dangerous."

"Of course they are," he agreed shortly, as if he didn't need her to give him a lecture. "But it's necessary to be a fine shot out here. In some ways your world would have been the same as my own. One tends to get taught everything. Ride, shoot, play tennis, even dance." He grimaced.

"I'm a very good chess player as well."

Was that wry admiration that flickered in his remarkable eyes?

"I don't doubt it. You'd excel at poker too, I would think. So I can safely take it you could handle a rifle if you had to?"

"If I had to." She nodded. "Rather a croc's funeral than mine. I don't hunt, before you ask. No sport whatever in that."

"I totally agree with you. We can safely rule the hunt out. I don't want to get on the wrong side of you. You tend to react as if you grew up with Queen Victoria. Now, are you coming with me, or not? I'm off to Melbourne first thing in the morning. Business. I won't be back until first thing Saturday morning."

"So when do your guests arrive?" No need to panic. She could handle an outback party. Lord knows she had organised splendid functions at the manor.

"Could you possibly sound anxious?" He couldn't resist the taunt, nor the near-overwhelming urge to pull free the yellow ribbon that tied back her billowing golden hair. It reached to her shoulder blades in sinuous curls and waves, unlike the evenings when she reverted to her smooth head-hugging arrangements.

"Do I *sound* anxious?" She put on her best formal tone.

"Actually, yes. I'm getting rather good at reading what goes on behind the high-born facade, Ms Balfour."

"That's a bit harsh, isn't it?" He flushed with vexation. "I have no inflated opinion of myself or my class."

"Of course you have," he said. "A whole battery of airs and graces. Some of them I like. But humility is clearly not your scene. Anyway, to get back to business. All of my guests will be flying in by midday Saturday at the latest. I'll be home by then."

"Would you mind putting that in writing?" she said, fighting for her habitual dignity.

He gave a low laugh. "Why, Olivia—I really like that name—my *word* is not enough?"

She felt as though she was on strange new ground. "It's just that I would like you to be here when your ex-wife and your daughter arrive." She wouldn't tell him she had the dismal notion Marigole would hate her on sight. For that matter so might Georgina, his troubled young daughter. Her father had never warned her about any of this, she thought bitterly. If things turned out very badly at Kalla Koori she didn't feel she could forgive him.

McAlpine suddenly caught her arm impatiently as though he had had quite enough of her backchat. Every time he did it she had to catch her breath. "Though I'm absolutely certain you can hold your own with anyone, Ms Balfour, I give you my word I'll be back before the others arrive."

She dared to give him a sideways glance. Their eyes held. Neither of them looked away. She *couldn't*. Much as he got under her skin—took delight in doing it—the man possessed fatal charm. It would throw any woman, even a woman of backbone like herself, off balance. Worse yet, it frightened her. She was a deeply reserved woman at heart.

Wasn't she?

Before she could react, he stretched out his hand and grasped her hair ribbon, setting the masses free.

She gave a mortified little cry while he watched with evident satisfaction as her hair cascaded around her agitated face. "Tell me, why do you feel the need to tie your hair back all the time?" He could see her fluster. Dusky pink coloured her cheeks, increasing the beauty she opted to play down. God knows why! "It's gorgeous hair. Darn nearly turns you into a femme fatale!"

He was making fun of her, of course. "Oh, stop that!" she ordered in queenly fashion, vigorously pushing her hair back over her shoulders. "It's *my* hair and don't you forget it. I like to be neat." She held out an imperative hand. "May I have my ribbon back?"

"Not today," he said briskly, jamming it into the breast pocket of his khaki bush shirt. "I know the stories about your grand manner are legion, Ms Balfour, but we're going to have to make an effort to modify it. Reveal the less starchy you. Otherwise you'll never get a husband. Now meet you outside in five minutes. We'll take the Range Rover. Don't forget your hat and your sunglasses."

In the act of hurrying away she turned back, blue eyes burning defiance.

"Kindly allow me to look after my own wardrobe, Mr McAlpine."

"Delighted to. Especially as it appears to be vast!" he shot back.

It was the most brilliant of days. Cloudless. So good, Olivia was starting to think she could love this place. Of course, it was hot—no denying that—and they had long records of cyclones, fires and floods, but it appeared to be taken by Territorians as

on-again, off-again events. It was simply the power of nature at
work. Even the fact that glassy-eyed saltwater monsters lurked
in the beautiful lily-festooned pools and lagoons was something
Territorians lived with on a daily basis. It didn't appear to worry
them. It was foolhardy tourists and the stupidly intoxicated most
likely to ignore all the warning signs—posted in several lan-
guages—who came to grief.

McAlpine kept up a running commentary which she had to
admit was both fascinating and engrossing. They had agreed
to "lay down our weapons," as he put it. It was oddly liberating. She had travelled much of the civilised world but Kalla
Koori was something else again. As was the force of McAlpine's
presence.

"This is the crocodile's natural habitat," he said. "Man is the
invader. From time to time there has to be a cull if they start
becoming too much of a threat, but we rather like our crocs."

"And to think they were probably around when the whole
continent was jungle. A *Jurassic Park* when the great reptiles
were dominant and the birds were only starting to appear."

He nodded. "The outback is famous for its birdlife. If we can
fit it in I'll take you to one of our Channel Country stations in
south-west Queensland. Legions of budgerigar without number
colour the sky green and gold. As for the prehistoric reptiles,
they may have disappeared—save for the croc—but we have
miniatures of the mighty reptiles in our lizards. The Japanese
in particular are fascinated by these little lizards. Even I think
they look fantastic with their armoury of spikes. We have the
frill-neck, the bearded dragons, thorny devil lizards, not to mention the geckos, snakes, goannas and skinks. You might as well
call the entire region the land of the lizards. Goannas can look
pretty fearless, especially when they rear up on the hind legs. The
perentie, our second largest to the Komodo dragon, can grow up
to seven feet and more."

They were driving across open boxwood-studded savannah,
with great flights of birds filling the sky with colour and raucous
calls. The sheer vastness of the landscape was having a powerful

effect on her. "In many ways I'm reminded of Africa," she said, "especially this never-ending sea of tall billowing yellow grasses. Look at the way they sway this way and that in the prevailing wind."

"African lions have the perfect camouflage in such grasses," he said. "Just little glimpses of the dense mane. I've been to South Africa several times. We have great friends in the Cape Colony and Natal. Magnificent creatures, lions, though I'm glad we don't have lion around here. We have quite enough to contend with. Those great spiky tussocks you see are the ubiquitous spinifcx. This is cattle country. No sheep."

"But you do have stations where you run both sheep and cattle." She felt more settled as he was clearly determined on being pleasant. She couldn't help knowing he found her—or her manncr—an irritant. She didn't actually like him either.

Did she?

"Read up a bit on us, have you?"

"Of course." So he was back to the sarcasm! She glanced out the window.

"Well, you might know, then, there are fourteen stations in the chain. They're spread right across the outback—the Queensland Channel Country with its mighty sand dunes and flood plains, the Kimberly in Western Australia and the Territory right up to the much cooler Barkly Tableland. I make it my job to look in on all of the stations and the permanent outstations like Naroo Waters from time to time."

She realised he was driving with care over the rougher spots. For her benefit she was sure; he wouldn't have done it on his own. He wasn't a complete barbarian. His aim obviously was to protect her from the worst jolting. "The Americans call your stations ranches?" She turned her head to question. Or could it be just another excuse to study his striking profile. He was an extraordinarily handsome and charismatic man. It would be unnatural not to imagine what he might be like as a lover. She was woman enough for that. But not woman enough to get involved. Such men were difficult to tame, let alone handle.

So be warned!

"We don't call our stations ranches." He glanced across at her, probably catching her out assessing him and the dangers he presented. "It was our early British settlers—the McAlpines among them—who called their vast pastoral holdings *stations*. It simply meant one was stationed or situated there. *Farm* is for something on a small scale, not a few million wild acres. *Station* was in common use right through the 1800s. We don't use the term *ranch*. It was the Americans who came up with *stampede*. Here a stampede is known—or was known—as a *rush* but *stampede* has caught on. One only has to live through one to appreciate how *stampede* says it."

"I don't believe I'll ever ask that question again," she said. "I'm on Kalla Koori Station."

"You are. Does that account for the little tremble?"

"What tremble?" She was worried he would notice. He had.

"Relax," he said. "You're perfectly safe with me."

She gave him a long look with her bluer-than-blue Balfour eyes. "I should jolly well hope so."

"Then there's no need to jump whenever I touch you."

"I do *not*!" she protested strongly. All the more so because he was right.

"Of course you do. Then you become as awkward as a novice nun."

"Well, I have to tell you I'm not used to men invading my privacy," she huffed.

He only laughed. "Lighten up, Olivia. What say we take a rest?"

"Why not!" she retorted shortly. Out in the open she might be able to breathe freely again. She knew he was baiting her. Worse, he enjoyed it.

They had been driving over his land for the best part of two hours. Mile after mile of vast empty distances, broken by broad streams of Brahman cattle, silver to dark grey in colour, en route to the nearest waterhole. Brahmans were better able to withstand tropical heat than European cattle, he'd told her. She could easily identify them from the distinctive large hump and the big droopy ears. Only a few stockmen appeared to be handling these large mobs. She couldn't imagine what might happen in a stampede.

"Brahmans are docile and intelligent animals," he said, "but they can on occasion be excitable. A lot of cross-breeding has gone on to up beef production. These days with the world in recession the public want cheaper cuts of meat. One of the reasons I sold off the central Queensland property to buy another in the Kimberly. With vast areas to cover, the cattle on the boundaries turn into very cunning rogues. They only have to pick up the slightest movement or sound and they scatter, finding shelter in the sand hills. Mustering unmarked cattle is very tough work. We won't ask you to do it."

"How do you know I wouldn't like to try? You underestimate me, McAlpine."

"I don't. Nor have I ever," he said bluntly, throwing her a glittering gaze.

That effectively shut her up.

From savannah, they were traversing a landscape of short green grass that looked for all the world like an infinity lawn. Millions of tiny wildflowers, mostly dark blue to purple with black white-flecked centres, rode the grass. Olivia rolled her window down to see if the wildflowers had any fragrance.

They did. "Oh, that's wonderful!" She breathed in their fresh floral fragrance.

"Native ground cover," he told her. "We can't match the sublime displays of wildflowers our Channel Country stations put on after the flood waters subside. And 2009 was a bumper year. Lake Lady Eyre in the Centre received a massive in-flow from our three great rivers system. The best flooding in living memory.

"Right now in case you're wondering, we're heading for a cluster of billabongs called Noola Lakes. Back in the Dreamtime, so the local legend goes, an arrogant young warrior named

Wapanga was captivated by a beautiful young girl of another tribe called Noola. Noola, promised to another, scorned him. Furious and humiliated Wapanga set fire to the dense scrub that surrounded the place where Noola was camped with her mother and sisters. The fire came down on them so fiercely and with such speed only Noola and two of her sisters were able to escape. When the fire was almost upon them Noola called out to the Great Spirits to help them with their magic. Whereupon she and her sisters were transformed into three lakes and Wapanga was turned into a black crow."

"And that's where we're going?" Her face, usually so composed, lit up.

Glancing at her, he realised he was taking a surprising amount of satisfaction from seeing her open up a little. Spread her petals as it were. Here was a genuine nature lover. Marigole had not been one for the bush, although right up to the time he had married her she had kept up an amazing pretence. Marigole was the mistress of devious behaviour.

"Oddly enough, you can always count on a single black crow hovering around the lakes." He gave the patrician Ms Balfour a half-smile.

To his surprise she returned it. It made him suck in his breath. She had a lovely smile. His hands on the wheel tightened imperceptively. Crisp-and-cool Ms Balfour could be a very sexy woman if she only knew it. Maybe she did know it and adopted the reserved front as the best way to deal with it. Her father had expected so much of her as his eldest daughter. Maybe too much.

The ground was becoming more marshy, Olivia saw. Strangely gnarled trees like living sculptures rose from shallow water. Around the trunks vivid green fernlike vegetation was sprouting, fanning out in great profusion.

"Noola Lakes are ponds of permanent fresh water," McAlpine said. "They have the great advantage of being safe. No salties lurk there, though I'm not recommending a swim today. It's simply a beautiful place on the station I want to show you. There are plenty of freshwater crocs in the Territory but they're not in the same league as the salties. About half their size, for a start, with a narrow snout. We consider them harmless to humans unless provoked."

"Well, I have no intention of provoking a single one of them," she said with an uncontrollable shudder. "I'm not given to rash deeds."

"My dear Ms Balfour, I would never have known."

She coloured. "How you do love to tease. Of course you're referring to my disgrace?"

"*What* disgrace," he said. "Was it such a great scandal after all? Personally I think Oscar has been a bit hard on his daughters."

"Maybe, but it wasn't my finest hour," she said quietly. "Bella and I just lost it."

"Everyone loses it from time to time, Olivia. I sure have. So don't keep beating yourself up about it. But surely it was Oscar who brought a lot of the trouble down on your heads. You and Bella meant well."

She released a grateful sigh. "Only Bella proved more compassionate than I. I will have to make it up to Bella though—we parted in floods of tears. One would have thought we were never going to see each other again instead of in a few months' time. I love my sister. I hated to row with her." She shook her blonde head rather miserably.

"Get over it," he said briskly. "What I saw of you and Bella, any number of rows wouldn't break the powerful bond. Oscar told me you had been an exemplary daughter and a most caring sister to your siblings."

"It wouldn't have hurt him to tell *me*," she said, shocked into showing her resentment. "I'm sorry. I shouldn't criticise my father. He's been wonderful to us all."

"Sometimes men forget to say what needs to be said."

Both of them were silent for several minutes pondering that.

"The land has a *religious* feel to it, hasn't it? A quality of time immemorial," she ventured.

Her perceptions, her sensitivity, pleased him a great deal, he suddenly realised. "Not so surprising when you think Australia is a most ancient continent. For the aboriginal people the land is sanctified ground." He threw her a long glance. Her beautiful skin was glowing, as were her blue eyes. She might have been Sleeping Beauty coming slowly out of her trance. "Some areas the elders regard as too holy to walk on."

They were on a winding track the colour of rust. "On the station?" she asked in surprise.

"We're talking an area of nearly four million acres," he said. "We can accommodate the holy spots. It's a primordial thing. It goes a lot deeper than Christian belief. The aboriginal tribes have been on this continent for more sixty thousand years as far as we know. They know the power of the land. They believe the land is not always benign. They have their Great Ancestral Beings. There are nurturing spirits and destructive spirits. A person's special essence, the soul, is a deeply held belief. Death and the afterlife are very important to them. Death is always associated with ritual, far longer and intense than our funerals and wakes. The elders on the station sing sacred songs daily. The chanting that went on after my father died—the sound of it, the wailing and the very real grief—will never leave me. To the aborigines on Kalla Koori my father has passed to the Sky World. He ascended on the bright rays of the setting sun." Despite himself he released a pent-up breath. He missed his father greatly.

Very gently she reached out to touch his arm. "I'm sorry. So sorry. I can see how much you loved him."

The muscles along his jaw line tightened. Her compassion had both surprised and moved him. "I admired him, respected him. He was a magnificent man. My mother adored him. It was a real love match. They don't happen as often as one might think."

"Well, good men are somewhat sparse on the ground," she observed with obvious regret.

He broke into a laugh. "Don't turn into a man-hater, Olivia."

"I can't afford to," she admitted. "I want children."

"And you'll make a good mother." She had been an admirable big sister. "May you be blessed with a round dozen. Better get a move on though. Your biological clock is ticking away. You're twenty-eight?"

"Not, I would have thought, over the hill," she said, incensed.

"Forgive me." The amusement was back. "Of course you've got time."

"You're at it again, are you? Can't stop yourself?"

"I'm just trying to loosen you up. Anyway, I'm no one to talk. All the marriages in our family have been very happy. Parents, grandparents, great-grandparents. Wonderful love matches that lasted. I broke the mould."

"Who said marriage was easy? You know my father has been married three times."

"If you can't make it at your third attempt I guess you never will," he returned sardonically. "Oscar appeared to have been very happy with his Lillian."

"She was a lovely, gentle person," Olivia said. "She never had good health. We all mourn her but I wouldn't be in the least surprised if my father remarries at some time in the future. He hasn't run out of...energy." She meant sexual as much as everything else. "People don't really change."

"I'm not about to agree. Not as yet. *You* won't know yourself by the time you're ready to fly home. Sometimes the mistakes we make in life serve to help us to see more clearly. Has any one man, outside your father, made you dreadfully unhappy?"

She gulped in a breath. "What do you mean, outside my father?" She wasn't ready to confront the whole issue head-on with this big, powerful Australian. "I love my father."

"Of course you do. But you did let it slip he wasn't always there for you."

She looked down at her hands. They were locked betrayingly in her lap. "I *do* recognise the fact he has always had to work extremely hard, as you made it your business to point out, but

I would imagine *you* as your father's heir were always kept in the loop. You were the heir apparent always in training. Men rule the world," she said with sharp disapproval. "It will never change."

"Oh, come on, Olivia!" he chided her. "More and more women in all parts of the world—where they're terribly oppressed and go in fear of their lives—are standing up and fighting from their corners. Even when they stand alone they cry out for freedom and justice. A lot of them are winning, as they thoroughly deserve to. More and more inspirational women are coming into the forefront of public life. That is as it should be. I grant you the revolution is taking overlong but a lot of women are perfectly happy to let men run the world for them. It's in the very nature of man to lead. In the nature of man to defend his own—his wife, children, family, country. Our women are joining the armed forces in greater numbers. They're needed. They have special skills. They go into the war zones, but the brass don't really want to risk pushing their young women into the front line."

"Even so, they get killed," she said sadly. "You think I've lived a useless, overindulged life, don't you?"

His expression was serious. "The more I get to know you, Olivia, the more I realise it hasn't been all that easy for you. But *you* know, as I know, you're capable of taking on much more fulfilling work than what you've been doing up to date. I wonder you haven't asked your father for a place in one of his many enterprises?"

"You think I haven't?" It was a cry from the heart.

"And he said *no*?" His brows drew together. Marigole had never shown the slightest interest in McAlpine business affairs. A big disappointment to him. Her only interest had been to spend the money, which she did so lavishly he had been forced to rein her in.

"I don't think he even heard me. It was sufficient for me to stay at home, perform my public duties and be there for my sisters. I was also on hand to act as his hostess when Lillian wasn't well enough, which was often."

"Poor little rich girl. One of the *jeunesse dorée*."

"The gilded youth. That's the way the paparazzi see us. Bella, in particular. She's so beautiful and glamorous and out there!"

"So that's why you play down your looks? So there's no competition between you and your twin?"

She was genuinely shocked. "There *is* no competition. Why ever would you say that? I'm quite happy to see Bella shine. Bella can make or break a function simply by turning up or not."

"I do understand Bella is the family wild child," he said. "The 'party queen'—don't the press call her that? I spoke to her at the wedding. She's very glamorous, but she's no more beautiful than you are. The most significant difference is your twin goes all out to dazzle, while you settle for a very dense smokescreen. Maybe it didn't help that you had to play big sister to your siblings? You should have been out and about enjoying yourself, not taking on much too demanding a role for your years and inexperience. Both of you could be crying out for attention and not fully realising it. Ever think of that?"

"If I have, I'm not about to say."

"Don't need to. Having everything material in life is no guarantee of happiness. I was blessed with a great childhood. I had all the love and stability in the world. That's a priceless advantage in life. I'm very worried about my daughter. Georgy used to be a quiet, studious, very respectful child. Sadly that's no longer the case. She's full of anger and she's taking less and less trouble to hide it."

Olivia started wondering if she was going to be on the receiving end of adolescent rages. "Perhaps she's still struggling with the divorce?"

"A powerful disruption. Sad to say, Georgy and her mother don't have a good rapport. It has everything to do with Marigole, not Georgina. Marigole is one of those women who dote on their sons. Such women can't seem to cope with daughters. Here, I think, Oscar shines. He loves you all. With my ex-wife and me, everything changed after Georgy was born. My family was thrilled with our perfect little girl. Marigole saw having a daughter as a failure. She wanted to bear a son and 'get it over.' Her words. She didn't want any more children. She found child-birth an excruciating experience never to be repeated."

"Perhaps she was frightened? Understandable."

"What she was frightened of was losing her figure," he answered grimly. "I'm telling you all this because you need to know. And there is the strong possibility someone along the way is bound to tell you."

"She can't be that shallow," Olivia, the feminist, retorted. "Maybe you couldn't love her the way she wanted?"

Try cutting him down to size.

"You're quite right, Olivia." He spoke as if applauding her. "I had a problem with that. We all want to love and be loved. That's what it's all about."

"Love does make the world go round." She wondered what it would be like to have an intense and loving communion with this man. Marigole was a bit of a mystery.

"It's our loved ones we strive for. Men throw themselves into their work to look after their families. Women run the home and take on part- and even full-time jobs. It's all for the common good. A man and woman plan their journey through life. I did believe myself in love with Marigole when I married her. I know you've got the wrong idea. It's in the condemnatory way you look at me out of those blue eyes. You can imagine my shock when the period of infatuation wore off. How did the beautiful, charming young woman I married turn into someone else? Was it *me*? Were my expectations too high? When I came to the full realization Marigole didn't love our daughter, it destroyed what was left. I hung in as long as I could. I had been brought up to believe marriage was for ever. But there was only one answer really. Divorce. We had to go our separate ways. Marigole doesn't want any more children. But I certainly do."

A swarm of butterflies fluttered in her breast. "A son, an heir?" What would it be like to go to bed with this man? Even the thought had the blood rushing to her head. To bear him a son! For a moment she was astounded at her own sensuality.

"A son, sure," he said. "But I'll take whatever heaven sends us."

"*Us?* You have a woman in mind?" In the inner most recesses of her heart how she envied this woman. It came as a revelation, profoundly shocking her. She didn't even *like* him.

Don't give us that!

"I hadn't until *you* showed up."

She was so stunned, she stuttered. "You c-can't mean... You c-can't be—" She broke off in utter confusion as she encountered the wicked glitter in his golden eyes. "Why do I always fall into the trap?"

"I don't know, Olivia." He gave her a twisted smile. "But you do."

CHAPTER FIVE

WHERE were they, the Garden of Eden before the fall? Olivia walked ahead of him, breathing in the crystal-clear air, so pure and bracing. This was the most romantic spot she had ever been in. The dappled sunlight on her upturned face was as warm and intoxicating as a kiss. Kiss? Kisses? Something had drastically altered her mindset. She was becoming extremely susceptible to the world of the senses. It had much to do with McAlpine. The sheer physical presence of him. She had the grace to admit that. He was the only man she had ever met who could dazzle her with his sexual radiance.

You should be very concerned about that.

She had taken her inner voice along for the walk with them.

For McAlpine's part, he appeared to be enjoying wandering around with her. That alone was giving her a huge buzz. Hugely unfamiliar for her—it had to be said. Surely her responses, however ill-advised, went a way to proving she wasn't frigid—or at least glacial. Hang on, *he* had called her that in Scotland. The cheek of him. Then as now the sheer audacity of the man took her breath away.

Of course, the tropical heat had to be factored in. It was luscious, thawing her cold-climate blood and causing her to act with unprecedented abandon. Before her, large brilliantly coloured butterflies sailed languorously. Her light footsteps crunched down on a thick ground cover of dry leaves, twigs and a wide scattering of tiny little wildflowers in the cool range of colours that showed their daisylike faces above the sandy white soil.

Everything seemed so much more vivid than usual. She thought the scene would be forever etched on her mind. That and the man who so nonchalantly was following her up. He might have been a lion on the prowl her heart was pounding so fast.

She realised she was moving a bit too quickly, getting way ahead of him instead of walking companionably alongside. Why? It wasn't a chase. She wasn't being pursued. Yet even the thought of a pursuit thrilled her. One could turn into a totally different woman with the right man. She was worrying that that man was McAlpine. She dared not get involved with him. But in its way it was rather wonderful to feel the way she did.

You could be courting disaster. Think about that.

Impossible to get away from the warning voice. Her father had sent her here to get a more insightful view of herself. In other words, find enlightenment.

Does anyone actually do that? Did Daddy for that matter?

All she knew was that she was undergoing a rapid change.

For better, or worse, Olivia?

Oh, shut up!

It seemed inconceivable to her so much lushness could co-exist with the sun-scorched grasses of the savannah and the terracotta plains. One could acquire a horde of worldly goods but nothing could compare with the matchless beauty and the deep spiritual power of nature. The full shade was blissful. Surely her wounded soul was on the mend? Her fall from grace had upset her more than anyone could know. That terrible row with her dearest Bella, her other half, her twin. Their rows had been so rare that the way they had gone at each other that terrible night—one might almost call it a catfight—had shocked them both to the core.

Even the thought of her twin made the tears spring to her eyes. But today the tears were mixed with delight. What had happened to her, what had happened to her family—the public disgrace—was starting to fade. Kalla Koori was a new world, a different universe. The whole atmosphere freed her up.

"This place looks pristine," she called back happily to McAlpine, waiting on his answer.

"Because of its extreme isolation." He watched her fling out her arm in a sweeping gesture, her expression so joyous he caught his breath. It was like seeing the petals of a budded pink rose slowly unfurl. Here was a woman ready to undergo a transformation. All she had to do was throw off the constraints of the past. A wedge of sunlight fell across her, turning her hair to spun gold. In her animation, she looked staggeringly beautiful. He had to take several deep breaths. Complications simply weren't on the agenda.

"Untouched since the Dreamtime!" Enchantment was in her voice. "I love that description—the Dreamtime—don't you? What a beautiful way to express it."

"I think so." He was still a short distance behind her, aware he was experiencing a lightness of spirit he hadn't felt in years. She might be overly conscious of her patrician background—a Balfour of Balfour Manor—but they shared similar feelings about a lot of important things. It was a source of deep gratification that she loved this place as he did. The beauty and power of nature had been quite beyond Marigole's understanding. Marigole only found herself in the big cities of the world.

All around them were beautiful trees of different heights and foliage. Olivia studied the striking patterns of the various barks. Most of these trees were unfamiliar to her. Towering palms trees dominated, some with slender trunks, others more substantial, grander. She saw several species of acacia. Great spiky pandanus trees and tall aquatic plants framed the crystal-clear ponds that lay at their feet. The ponds now in clear view were surprisingly large, isolated one from the other by stretches of pure white sand and intermittent silver-grey boulders.

"Lubra Lakes." An element of excitement was in her voice. She understood immediately this was a special place. Mystical in character. Each great pond glittered with a mirrorlike intensity, the colour a uniform deep emerald green. Some of the grace-ful gums that bent their heads over the pools were draped with vines bearing exquisite red-orange throated flowers that were so sweetly scented she thought the fragrance ought to be bottled.

"Enjoying yourself?" His tone was indulgent.

"I'm having a great time." She turned back to him, her normally contained expression lifted into radiance. "This is the loveliest place. We might be visitors to an ancient cathedral."

"Which is why I brought you here." He moved with surefooted grace down the coarsely grassed slope. "Tell me, do you still feel punished for being sent here?"

She felt her cheeks pink. "Actually, I'm asking myself why I ever worried."

You should!

OK, she had to trust in her common sense. There was no future in this adventure as far as she could see. She was to return home. McAlpine would remarry, hopefully this time happily. She was as sure as she could be of anything that he wouldn't have his work cut out finding another wife. Apart from the obvious wealth, he was such an arresting man with a presence and air of command that went far beyond his years. His powerful body, so athletic, gave off remarkable energy. In that way he fitted into the same mould as her father. Both of them magnetic men.

Even thinking it, she was overcome by an extraordinary indolence. She didn't wonder at its source. He was standing right beside her. She wanted to crumple gracefully onto the sand, then lay back against its yielding warmth. Once there she would fix her eyes on him…lift a hand, beckon him, allurement in her eyes. She knew with every fibre of her being she could count on him to be everything a woman could want in a lover. She had given up hoping for that. In Scotland, increasingly thrown off balance by him, she had decided wrathfully he was anything but her type. How different it was here, on his own land.

Your physical attraction to him was always there.

Now came profound understanding.

Her inner voice crashed in with a warning.

Do you honestly think you'd be a match for him?

Probably not. But no other man had put her in a fever, or

caused a tsunami of sensation. She was floundering in the giant swells.

"So what *did* you have to worry about?" McAlpine was asking. His expression suggested he recognised she was falling out of character. Or the cool, self-assured character she liked to present to the world.

Are you going to pull yourself together?

She chose not to listen. Instead she inhaled deeply, bending to pluck a wildflower. "I did entertain a few concerns we mightn't get on. That and the prospect of loneliness, of course. The station is very isolated, vast and near *empty* of humans. I've been thinking of how the men and women on the First Fleet must have felt when they arrived in the Great South Land. A glorious blue harbour to confront them, but beyond that an enormous wilderness—an island continent unlike anything they had ever seen—only a handful of miles beyond their small settlement the impassable Blue Mountains. I call that daunting. I come from a small overcrowded island. Enormous open spaces such as you have here can be overwhelming. My life has been so very different."

"Very structured," he agreed. "But please don't forget it was the men and women of the tiny British Isles that opened up this vast country and colonised it. My ancestors among them. That took real guts." He removed the pretty little wildflower from her hand, then pushed it into her hair. "You're not afraid of *me*, are you?"

"In a way." She wouldn't have to work hard to turn him into the object of a hopeless passion.

Don't show agitation. It means nothing. He doesn't fancy you. This crazy rush of emotion is all on your side.

"What way?"

She didn't know how to respond.

"Olivia?"

She shook back her hair, dislodging the flower. "Nothing serious. But I know I irritate you and you can't deny it."

His eyes gleamed pure gold. "All human beings irritate one

another from time to time. I'm more *impatient* of the fact you underestimate yourself and your worth. The more I get to know you, the more I see beneath the ultra-cool pose, where may well lay chronic loneliness. You could throw in a dollop of insecurity."

He was looking at her steadily, openly challenging her, but she could only feign a nonchalant shrug. "You must have defective reasoning powers if you think I'm lonely or insecure." It seemed imperative to get back to her old form.

He appeared to acknowledge just that. "Olivia, I don't want you to feel threatened by anything I say. I'm merely pointing out you spend a lot of time protecting your image. Be yourself. That's my advice. Your real self, like you are today. Don't shut life out. It has to be lived. We shouldn't die pondering and mourning all the things we didn't do for want of a certain courage. Reach out. Few amongst us haven't been hurt, but we have no option but to live in hope."

She could tell him she wasn't managing to shut *him* out. He was getting to her at every level. Her hitherto impregnable defences were proving as flimsy as a set of cardboard boxes. "Shutting people out goes along with a fear of betrayal."

"Tell me about it!" There was an edge to his voice. "So who are *you* talking about here, an ex-lover? Wasn't there someone in tow at the wedding? I seem to remember a blond guy hovering in the background undecided whether to break up our little altercation or not."

"That was Justin," she said. "I'd become resigned to the fact I couldn't seem to sustain relationships. Now it occurs to me I didn't actually *want* to. I suppose that's a step along the road to self-enlightenment, would you say?"

"Sure is. So you haven't been in love?"

To her astonishment she answered truthfully. "Thought I was. But not for long."

"Do you believe in love at first sight?"

She believed in a storm of emotion. "Did you fall in love with your ex-wife on sight?" she countered. He probably had. Won-

derful sparks right from the start. Something like she had experienced with him. Only they were sparks of sexual hostility.

"I'd known Marigole since we were kids. But as for the leg-
endary *coup de foudre*, that hasn't hit me. Tell me about Justin."
He stooped to pluck another purple wildflower. "Is he in or out?"
He straightened, pushing the flower into her abundant golden
hair, then standing back to admire the effect. "No, don't touch
it," he said, as she put up a tentative hand.

"I was only going to tuck it in more firmly. I didn't mean to
throw away the last flower. It's just that you have a way of rattling
my cage."

"And it's dead easy. Why is that?"

The expression in his eyes appeared intense. "Because you're
Australian," she said, offering an idiotic explanation. "Oh, God,
let me rephrase that. You're very frank. We British are inclined
to be much more reserved."

"You consider that a *good* thing?" He didn't bother to point
out his family's British background. She would have known it
anyway.

The fear of being mesmerised increased her desire to protect
herself. "It's always been *my* approach."

"Could be one reason why you've led such a dull life. And
you have had a dull life, haven't you, Olivia, for all the material
splendour? When we first came down here your responses were
uncomplicated, spontaneous. Let's stick to that."

"You're the boss!"

"And you can't ignore it," he said with a glint in his eyes.

She was grateful for the feather-light breeze that was cooling her
flushed cheeks. It was a relief to turn away from his searching
eyes. Eyes that seemed to divine she was an emotional mess. Each
day it was becoming more apparent to her that the person she
had striven so hard to create, the person she thought her father
wanted, didn't match up with her inner identity at all. McAlpine,
almost a stranger, had plumbed that fact.

Why do you let him rouse you? Rouse you and rouse you. Not just your body. Your soul.

Maybe she was evolving far too fast.

The whole area was alive with bird song, punctuated by the odd startling cry. She continued on, to be nearer the water. The perimeter of each lake was festooned in glorious native water lilies. Very curiously with floating lilies of a different colour— one a gorgeous blue-violet, another the palest yellow with a gold-brown centre, the third so deep a pink they were almost lilac.

"Was the planting deliberate?" she turned back to ask in a conciliatory manner. If he suddenly disappeared she would be totally lost in this flowering wilderness. "Different coloured lilies in each lagoon?" She didn't want to fall out with him. She wanted them to be friends.

Who are you fooling? Don't you really mean, much more than friends?

He moved slowly towards her, looking amused. "Olivia, the blue lotus is found naturally all over our tropics. It's common to Australia and North Africa. It was the sacred flower of ancient Egypt, as you probably know. Most of our pools and lagoons carry flowers of the one colour. After the rains on our stations in the Queensland Channel Country you have mile after mile of white everlastings that eventually run into mile after mile of yellow."

"How lovely!" She was standing only a few feet from the edge of the emerald water. Shards of sunlight were hitting the transparent wings of dragonflies, iridescent blue and dark yellow as they darted from one stunning water lily to the other. "Are there fish in the lakes?"

"Nothing to make a meal of. In season the lakes are a haven for all manner of water birds, including the black swans. Be careful where you're walking now." The grass had turned coarse and grainy.

"I'm fine." She was fairly suffocating with sexual awareness. In fact, he made her feel so hot she could break out in a rash. The tiniest miscalculation on her part and she could make an utter fool of herself. She feared that above everything. Staying in control had been an important component of her character. She knew she was incapable of handling a man like McAlpine.

Poor old Justin was more your speed.

How she would love to distance herself from that inner voice! It was even possible she had an over-reliance on it. Bella had no inner voice to prevent her from taking things to what she in her righteousness had often considered *extremes*. Maybe Bella had the better way of doing things?

There was a sudden loud, whirring sound. The beating of dozens of wings. She looked up to witness a great flock of brilliantly coloured parrots coming in to settle in the trees. She stood magnetised by the spectacle, throwing back her head to glory in the sight. The sun flashed off strong jewel colours— emerald, ruby, sapphire, topaz, garnet. Her head was flung so far back she felt a flicker of vertigo. To counteract it, she reached for a low-hanging branch, conveniently to hand. Only at the very moment she clutched it, it gave a sharp crack, then snapped off in her hand.

She let out a muffled cry, afraid she was going to skid down the bank into the water, crushing the carpet of native herbs as she went.

Only McAlpine was there to catch her.

Surreal! How had he done that?

A pouncing lion couldn't have made it faster.

"Bravo!" There was a self-congratulatory note in his voice. They might have been a pair of trapeze artists and he had just saved her from a nasty nosedive.

One arm was locked around her waist in a steely embrace. She couldn't stand straight. It was as if she had entered a state of total paralysis that compelled her to remain bent over his arm. Her two good legs offered no support whatever. Another huge difficulty was to get back her breath. Even the chatter of the birds had stilled in anticipation of her next move.

He turned her body, glowing now, in his arms. She couldn't

bear to look at him. The tight leash she habitually kept on herself had snapped. Were there no bones in her legs at all?

"Olivia?"

Was there a thread of mockery beneath the concern? She felt like whimpering. Wouldn't that be shocking to whimper at the ripe old age of twenty-eight! There didn't appear to be an iota of strength left in her body. God knows what a doctor would have to say about her condition. She only knew she was without enough breath to respond. Her hair had let her down as well. It was in total disarray, flowing everywhere, like it used to do when she was a child.

Surely this confirms you're sexually repressed?

The danger was her *real* self fighting to get out.

Her mind might have been scrambled, but her body began to obey some fundamental need. It started to press into his. Male against female. Shocking, sensual pleasure. In one way she felt stunned; in another, the strange feeling was approaching euphoria. She imagined powerful circuits switching on in her brain…lighting up…dopamine pouring into her blood… He might have been kissing her all over.

Moments were stretching into infinity. Even McAlpine seemed to have lost direction. Her breasts rose and fell in agitation, nipples hard as berries. Human sexuality wasn't all that different to the animal kingdom. Male and female were designed to mate. It wasn't long intellectual discussions that brought it about. It was action. And action had been missing from her life.

He spoke first, his voice as smooth and golden as warm honey. "What can a man do when he finds a beautiful woman in his arms?"

Dredge up what's left of your control, girl. Go on.

The voice was whispering as though it was all it could do to issue the husky warning.

She didn't want to *go on*. God, his hands were grasping her hips. But she knew she had to make an attempt. "He could let her go," she said into the fraught pause. She couldn't think straight.

Her stomach was doing somersaults in the way of a woman getting ready for a parachute jump.

"I will in a moment." He was making best use of that mellifluous mesmerising voice. "It's just that I have a hunch you badly need kissing. Not now and again, but constantly. I'm good with my hunches. Raise your head, Olivia. Be daring for once in your life."

The challenge put her on her mettle. Overbearing, arrogant, incredibly sexy man. He needed putting in his place. "Don't even think of kissing me," she warned in her cut-glass voice.

He pulled back a fraction. "For a goddess to be scared of mortal man?"

"Scared? Good gracious, I'm not scared of *you*, McAlpine." Scared of all the disturbances within her maybe.

"Scared of yourself, then?"

Spot on.

She threw up her head. "Look, I'm not getting into any situation when I'm forced to spend months with you."

His expression was suave. "But my dear Ms Balfour, I wouldn't dream of taking advantage of you. I'm probably more of a gentleman than your insipid Justin."

"He's *not* my Justin."

"Glad to hear it. I thought he was a real wimp. You deserve a lot more. What we need to find out is what has gone wrong in the past. Why your love affairs haven't worked."

"*You* should talk!" she shot back, blue eyes flashing.

"I agree. But maybe that's why I feel for *you*. First we need to know whether you can kiss. That's a start. I have an idea you favour keeping your strawberry lips tightly shut."

"Having fun, are we?" she asked loftily.

"I'm dead serious, Olivia. You're twenty-eight. High time you were married. I know you want kids."

"Surely that's normal enough," she returned with considerable heat. "I'm normal enough."

"Let's find out." He moved her in closer.

God, girl! Time to act. Pour scorn on him. Freeze him out.

Hard to freeze anyone when you felt molten. "I'm thinking you're a shameless man."

"For wanting to kiss you?" His voice deepened.

"You *want* to kiss me?" She drew in a convulsive breath.

"You're in my domain." He slid his arms down her straight back to her waist.

"I'm well aware of that. But I came here on business, remember?" What her body desired was way too dangerous.

"Nonsense! Your dad shunted you out of the country. There's a huge scandal on the front page of the world's newspapers every other day of the week. You know that as well as I. It's all part of the media cycle. Illegitimate children abound. Who worries about that any more? Children are a great blessing. Anyway, everyone gets their fifteen minutes of blame. I promise you, Olivia, this little experiment will be painless."

She felt maddened by their proximity. "I don't take kindly to experiments."

"Trust me. I'm on *your* side. You fascinate me. You did from our first frosty encounter. Of recent times I've come to the conclusion you don't actually know *how* to come down from your pedestal."

"And you're happy to hold the stepladder?" Her knees were sagging beneath her.

"Well, I've had far more experience than you. Why not pass a little of that expertise on. The big plus for me is you have such a beautiful, sensitive mouth."

A sound like static was crackling in her ears. "Subtext—I don't know *how* to use it to kiss? Is that what you're saying?" She tried to disengage. Couldn't. "My answer to your little experiment has to be no, McAlpine. I'm sure you don't hear *no* often. This is one of your experiments that won't work."

"Only I'm thinking it will." He was holding her as though he relished having her in his arms.

Would you just look at that challenging glint in his golden eyes! Are you going to stand for it?

More likely she was about to cast off her old moral code.

"You're a seriously arrogant man."

"I'm one of the good guys. I've suffered, Olivia. Just like you."

All of a sudden her tender heart smote her. She was a woman who took no pleasure in people's suffering. Even McAlpine. The acknowledgement that he had suffered sent her last defence crashing. Behind the all-conquering male front, he too could be in need of comfort.

Comfort wasn't what she got. Or gave. Rather a raging excitement. Regrets could come later. She found herself breathing in the scent of him like a woman deprived of an essential powerful aphrodisiac. So extravagant was her reaction to it, she began to lose touch with the world around her. There was no drawing back, no flinching, no timidity—only wave after wave of pleasure. His mouth—such a firm generous mouth—came down on hers not hard or fast, but slowly…slowly…savouring the taste of her as though she was utterly delectable. It was astonishing to experience the wild burst of freedom. No need for him to prise her lips apart with the tip of his tongue. He had instant admittance. She who had earned a reputation for being cold had finally discovered the one man to turn up the heat.

The kisses altered in character…deepened, bringing forth her soft moans. "Your skin is like satin…as cool." He turned his ministrations to her face, dragging his mouth across her cheekbones, her cheek, letting his lips trail down the column of her neck. A normal enough communication in lovemaking, only the way he did it was so erotic she had to bite her lips to prevent herself from crying out. The static in her ears was turning into a roar, like waves crashing up against a cliff.

"Clint?" Her voice quavered. He had to relent or she would be totally seduced.

He kissed her mouth again before answering. "You want me to stop? Or do you want me to really make love to you?"

She couldn't mistake the powerful tension in him or his male arousal. He wasn't nearly as much in command of himself as he might like to think. She reached to grasp his wrist. "What are we doing?" she asked frantically. This was no experiment. This was full-on sexual passion. "You're not in love with me. You don't *know* me. I don't know you."

"Then how come we're doing so astoundingly well?" He stared challengingly into her eyes. "I don't play childish kissing games, Olivia. I *do* feel something for you. That's pretty obvious. You feel something for me, so don't bother to deny it. But you're right. No seduction scene allowed. Just a sizzle. And I thought I was off women, would you believe?"

"Men of strong passions don't go off women," she said bluntly, thinking of her father.

Thump…thump…thump. Her heart was drumming so hard she had to hold a hand to it. He had aroused her to such a pitch. And so *easily.* God knows what would happen if they ever got into bed.

He released her, holding up his palms in a gesture of surrender. "Well, you've certainly mastered the kiss and in only one lesson. What say we try again before we go to be sure? I'm fully aware you're here on business, only this time give me all you've got."

Her temper shot up in plumes of flame.

Give it all you've got!

She was so furious, she *did.*

The second time it was like plunging into a volcano with a billion lava-red stars to light up the darkness. She felt weightless. Except for her breasts that by comparison felt heavy. There was also an intense quivering between her legs, little knifelike plunges. She tried to clench her muscles to make it stop. It only made it worse. The action was painfully and massively erotic. And he was only *kissing* her. What if he started working her out of her clothes? What if he started kissing the most erogenous zones of her body? She didn't know if she could stand the liberation. On the other hand, she was responding like a woman breaking out of a suffocating cocoon.

You were dying for this!
I know.
Only you could be giving your heart away. Remember, Houseman? Give crowns and pounds and guineas but not your heart away.

The abruptness with which he released her was startling. Mercifully he kept a hold on her shoulder because she was swaying like a willow in a high wind.

He gave her a taut half-smile. "That will do for today. Though to my mind, your education is complete."

"Well, you'd know, McAlpine." Her legs were wobbly, her breath unsteady.

"You can't manage *Clint*?"

"McAlpine helps keep me on my guard."

"You'll have to call me Clint when my guests arrive." He studied her with interest. Her blue eyes were ablaze, the cool classical features softened into an alluring womanliness. "Better go back to the jeep?" he said.

Before all control was lost.

She followed his cue, her manner, ludicrously under the circumstances, formal. "Thank you for showing me this wondrous place."

"I trust you to come down here by yourself. I've accepted your word you're an experienced rider." She would be with her upbringing.

"Nothing to stop you from checking me out."

He gave her his hand as the going got rough. "We'll make it late this afternoon. I can fix you up with the right mount and saddle. I'd like you to wear a hard hat when you're out. At least until you get to know the terrain. It would take us days to drive around the station. We've stayed close in, where I want you to remain."

"Your wish is my command." He could easily have let her hand go, yet he continued to hold it, smothering her in feeling. "Do you suppose your daughter will like me?"

"You want her to?"

"Of course." She removed her tingling hand as they reached the top of the slope. "I don't suppose your ex-wife will. Mightn't it be a good idea if I called you Mr McAlpine while she's around?"

"We don't go in for such formality around here, Olivia. Clint is fine. My ex-wife has a new man in her life. With any luck at all she'll marry him."

"What *is* love?" she asked.

His expression turned bleak. "Whatever it is, Olivia, it's in pretty short supply."

Saturday morning Olivia was up at first light. She was nervous, although she'd had a great team to support her during the week— no lukewarm responses such as she'd been guilty of herself in the past, but enthusiastic approval. It occurred to her she had lived her life encased in her own private space. That wasn't happening here. The team wanted in. Her "posh" accent brought forth many a chuckle from the house girls, as though she was doing a lot of it for fun.

Bessie came and went as she pleased. She was treated with great respect as befitting a tribal princess. This week she had returned from a painting trip into the desert, presenting Olivia with her first piece of what was a unique blend of aboriginal and western art. The canvas depicted a field of wildflowers, their faces with wonderful definition. Great storm clouds were massed in the background; in the foreground an aboriginal rain maker, naked except for a few strategic feathers, going about his ancient ritual, holding aloft a long stick which Bessie told her was a yamstick, always associated with magical powers.

"This *is* magic, Bessie." Olivia felt moved to tears by such a splendid gift.

"Them fellas do the magic. I've seen 'em make rain. The downpours make the desert bloom. All those wildflowers I paint are botanically correct."

"I'm sure they are. Thank you so much, Bessie. I love it. I'll take it home with me when I go. Value it always."

"That's if we let yah escape!" Bessie gave a big smile, show-ing her beautiful teeth. "Your heart has opened up, Livvy. You might not get to leave us at all."

Again Olivia thought she was privy to a prophecy.

So many times in the past she had been challenged to show off her skills as her father's hostess. Heaven knows she had done the rounds of all the major social events—the Balfours were invited everywhere—as well as formal and informal dinner parties. She had always felt confident of orchestrating a dinner party for anything up to forty people. She had made it her business to foresee everything her father might want and he was a very exacting man. Which people were fun, interesting, socially con-nected, influential, including those that were at the top of the political game.

Kath had been a tower of strength, making her famous bitter-chocolate mousse tart which Olivia had pronounced superb at their trial run. There was a time-honoured Moroccan orange tart—almost as delicious—for those who professed to have had their fill of chocolate. Honestly, could that happen? For start-ers she planned oysters in champagne with caramelised spring onions. For those who didn't like oysters, there were artichoke hearts with foie gras.

Because she had spent so much time in Morocco and McAlpine knew it well, she and Kath had perfected a tagine of chicken with preserved lemon. It was to be served with piping-hot rice and garnished with tiny sprigs of watercress. She'd had lots of fun choosing the wines from an extensive cellar, of imported and domestic product. Nothing but the best!

Kath had thoroughly enjoyed being put on her mettle. The four house girls, with Bessie making up a highly vocal and sharp observer, were fascinated by the whole procedure. The house was full of the most beautiful flowers. The orchids that had been flown in from Thailand had cost an arm and a leg.

"You've got carte blanche!" McAlpine had assured her before he left.

"You sure know how to do things, Livvy," Bessie gazed with pleasure around the formal dining room. "I never seen a dinner table look so beautiful. Clint's mum and his aunty Buffy are known for their gracious tables. Just between you me and the gatepost, they've met their match."

Olivia had to blush. The team were so full of unstinting praise. It would be terrible to come a cropper. Especially with the ex–Mrs McAlpine around. "I'm good at some things, Bessie," she confided, perfecting the placement of a table setting. "Not terribly good at others."

"Get away with yah!" said Bessie. "All you'll ever need to be is yahself." She rubbed her palms together as though the friction was the first move in creating a spell. "So what are you gunna wear?" she asked with interest, surveying Olivia's ultra-slim figure. Olivia was wearing one of her silk shirts with linen trousers, her hair pulled tight off her face into a Grecian knot.

"Lord knows! I may need some advice." Bessie had proved herself as a wonderfully artistic person. She had a great eye for colour.

"Just don't go scraping yah hair back," Bessie advised "Not that it ain't nice. But for evenin'! I just love your hair. When it's out you look like a princess in a fairy tale."

"Except I don't really go in for glamour, Bessie."

"That's because you're always hidin'," said Bessie. "Yah can't stifle the person yah really are, Livvy. Not forever. I bin dreaming about yah!" Bessie's liquid gaze was deep and mysterious. "I wanna see those dreams come true."

CHAPTER SIX

TRUE to his word, McAlpine was back at the homestead by 10:30 a.m. He strode along the portico feeling like a man with a renewed zest for life, entering the house in time to see the strange yet intensely familiar Ms Olivia Balfour tweaking an extravagant arrangement of flowers that wouldn't have been out of place in the lobby of the Bangkok Oriental. True to her patrician style, she had commandeered the magnificent Chinese fish bowl that stood on its rosewood stand and filled it with every flower under the sun. He recognised masses of Oriental lilies, orchids of many varieties—flights of *phalaenopsis* like quivering butterflies, sprays of purple *dendrobiums*—Queensland's state flower, roses, grasses, ferns, branches, lotus pods, you name it. No one had ever used the very valuable eighteenth-century fish bowl before for flower arrangements. Not even his mother. He had to say the effect was little short of sumptuous which wouldn't have been a difficult task for a Balfour of Balfour Manor.

"How much did that little lot set me back?" He had to fight off the strong compulsion to catch her up and kiss her. Why not, considering their mind-blowing physical reaction to each other at Lubra Lakes. What had prompted him to kiss her? He had known perfectly well he was playing with fire and it didn't exactly tally with his claim he was off women. Still he had steamed ahead. Even more of a folly was that she had never been out of his mind for the past few days. In fact, Ms Olivia Balfour had turned his ordered world upside down. It stunned him.

And yet! He had never felt so alive.

Olivia, for her part, turned her head slowly, pretending calm, when she ached with excitement. Even the sound of his voice caused her heart to go into overdrive and every cell in her body to vibrate. "I hoped you'd like it," she said coolly, falling back on her long training. "Would you like to give the dining room and the reception rooms the once-over? My father always does."

"By all means!" he answered crisply as he joined her. Why the hell didn't he entwine her in his arms? She had to be nervous because she began to check her immaculate hairdo. "Let's emulate Oscar. He recognised your value way back as a chatelaine. I'm sure he never meant to, but he treated you more like a wife than a daughter. Look after the children, run the manor and the various houses around the world, organise all the dinner parties, open the garden parties and the fetes, look after the charities, action groups, whatever!"

He had the shocking ability to hit on raw truths. Hadn't the very same thing crossed her mind more than once, before being swiftly banished as disloyalty?

"All my life I've worked to be the person my father wanted me to be," she confessed. "He always spoke of a father's unconditional love but we all knew certain conditions went along with that love."

He smiled wryly. "So now you're coming around to thinking you've spent your life stifling the person you really are?"

"But that's what you want me to think, isn't it?"

"Don't let's waste time, Olivia. I do."

"Well, at Balfour Manor, *chatelaine* is a very prestigious position."

"There are better ways to go," he pointed out sardonically.

"Did your business affairs go well?" She broke the lengthening silence. Why did he make her feel so foolish?

"They did, Ms Balfour. Thank you for asking."

He gave her that mocking smile. Such an illumination of his handsome features that could sometimes look stern. She sucked in her breath, fluttery feelings in her chest and stomach. All the time he'd been away she had caught herself up, fantasising about having sex with this man. No one could have been more surprised than herself. She'd had the odd daydream in the past. Nothing like what was happening to her now.

Pitiful, Olivia. A huge mistake.

It wasn't smart to ignore the voice in one's head. Generally speaking it only gave good advice. The big trouble was, her *body* spoke a different language. McAlpine would be an adventurous, blindingly passionate lover. Very erotic. Her scant handful of lovers had never ventured past the time-honoured—maybe outdated?—missionary position. Every instinct screamed that McAlpine would run the gamut of positions that were mutually, ravishingly arousing.

She had to shake herself out of yet another reverie.

"All most ethical," he was saying with satisfaction. "I'm stretching my horizons, Olivia. I want you to do that too. Get into new things. As far as business goes, even in the huge global downturn, there are strategies to keep afloat."

"Well, my father seems to think you're someone extraordinary," she said, allowing the note of hauteur to creep back into her voice again. The last thing she could afford was to have him know he was occupying just about all her thoughts. It wouldn't win her any points with his ex-wife and his daughter either to appear smitten.

"Can't leave you alone for long, can I?" His gleaming eyes were brim full of mockery.

"I beg your pardon?"

"Simple, Olivia. You're back to the divine aloofness. And you do it superbly. So tell me, what are you wearing this evening? Your best black?"

Best black! If there was one thing she hated it was a man who could read her mind. Suddenly her best black lost its appeal. "Perhaps I'll surprise you," she said tartly.

"That's great! I so look forward to seeing different aspects of your personality emerge."

"I have you under observation as well." She turned away to adjust a dried lily pod that looked perfectly fine the way it was. "What right do you have to be so patronising about my wardrobe?"

"Not patronising, Olivia. I want to help you. I thought we'd agreed you would look upon me as your mentor."

"I don't know that I agreed to that!"

"Oh, you agreed all right," he said very drily. "So don't let me down."

"Perish the thought! Shall we continue on our rounds?" she asked briskly.

He gave her a droll look. "By all means, Matron." He gestured with his hand for her to lead on.

She called on her old claim to fame. Coolness under pressure. Blonde head held high she began to stalk away from him. "Thank God I'm only here for a few months."

"Just bear in mind others have had an epiphany in less time," he called, admiring the swish of hips and long slender legs. Ms Olivia Balfour would be a match for any man.

McAlpine's guests, obviously not short of a shilling, began arriving by light aircraft not all that long later. Neil and Celine Jameson, a pleasant young couple; Peter and Barbara Corbett, who greeted her in a warm friendly manner; Brendan Fraser, McAlpine's close friend, with a knockout young redhead many years his junior, Chloe, on his arm. Olivia recalled Kath's description of him as the "perennial bachelor." She also recalled he was the one who had called the ex–Mrs McAlpine a she-devil. What a ghastly description! Did Marigole really deserve it? She had the weekend to find out.

Brendan was tall, rugged, with a zesty way about him that made people laugh and relax. Olivia didn't overlook the high intelligence and the piercing shrewdness in the humorous dark eyes. She didn't have the slightest doubt Brendan had started summing her up from the moment they had been introduced. Obviously he was very protective of his lifelong pal. Not that McAlpine needed any protection. But men stuck together. That was the way of it.

The last to arrive, predictably, as Kath had warned her in advance, were Marigole, her daughter, Georgina, and Marigole's new man in her life, Lucas Harcourt.

Everyone and everything had fallen so neatly into place, small wonder Olivia thought something just had to go wrong. It wasn't such a great surprise, then, when it did.

Marigole McAlpine was just about as unfriendly as one woman could get with another. After a tip-to-toe rake of Olivia's elegant figure, she assumed the expression of a woman intent on a cold war. No question, the ex–Mrs McAlpine still had an extremely proprietary attitude towards the man she had divorced.

Oh, right! She is *a she-devil.*

"How do you do, Ms Balfour." Marigole, who appeared to have a great sense of fashion, fixed Olivia with an icy stare. Not all that easy with enormous dark eyes. They dominated a milky white face of small perfect features that somehow added up to hard. She might have suspected Olivia guilty of sleeping with her betrothed instead of her ex-husband.

And you're not sleeping with him.

More's the pity.

"Clint said nothing about your being here." A rebuke was implicit in her tone.

"Didn't know I had to." McAlpine entered the conversation, one arm wrapped around his daughter's shoulder. He was hugging her close and she was looking up at him adoringly. Olivia had an instant picture of herself with her father at Georgina's age. The expression was pretty much the same. "Olivia is the daughter of one of my most valued business partners," McAlpine was saying.

"Not *Oscar* Balfour?" Lucas Harcourt's thick eyebrows shot up and the bonhomie he radiated escalated an extra notch. An urbane man in his early fifties, slightly rotund, he had a lined, clever face and a full head of silver-grey hair he was lucky to hold on to considering the paucity of other physical assets.

"My father." Olivia smiled. Lucas, although he had given her a close but discreet inspection, was very much the gentleman, with a good firm handshake—just the right measure of formality—she liked. She didn't mind Lucas at all. Marigole at close quarters was the sort of woman she normally avoided like the plague. Yet such women men seemed to find irresistible. She had seen it time and again. Loved him. Hated her. It did happen.

"Good Lord," said Lucas, his lined, scored face lighting up. "Now there's a man I'd like to meet."

"I'm sure when you're in London it can be arranged." Olivia gave Georgina, who had said nothing beyond a muttered "hello," an inclusive smile. She was a beautiful child. The image of her mother. Huge dark eyes, straight dark hair tumbling like a satin bolt down her back. One could only hope she hadn't inherited her mother's less than sweet nature. Considering her wealthy background Georgina looked painfully awkward, a mixture of shyness, insecurity and possibly a lot of seething inner rebellion.

"Kath has lunch scheduled for one-thirty," Olivia told them, not overly bothered by Marigole McAlpine. She had met a lot worse. The Honorable Alice Beaufort for starters, and her marginally less offensive sister, Camilla. "So if you'd like me to show you to your rooms?" Olivia threw out a graceful hand.

"Don't bother," Marigole retorted rudely. She turned to her ex-husband, waving one arm about as though she was fighting to find just the right words. "You didn't say Ms Balfour is here as your assistant."

"Lots of things I haven't mentioned, Marigole." McAlpine's answer was sardonic. "Do lighten up. Olivia is here on a study tour. She very kindly offered to act as hostess for the weekend and the various functions I have coming up. Buffy is out of action, I'm sorry to say."

Marigole's glossy bob swung back to Olivia, with a look that clearly said, *And I hope you screw up big time!*

"Extraordinary man, your father," Lucas was remarking, rubbing his chin thoughtfully and returning to his theme. "Balfour! Now that's a name synonymous with style and glamour." He gave Olivia's tall elegant figure a look of positive admiration.

"I'm assuming we're in the same suite, Clint?" Marigole cut in, her expression reflecting a bottomless well of black thoughts.

"But of course!" McAlpine exclaimed, giving his daughter another hug. "You didn't think I was going to move you into a hotel?"

Georgina was betrayed into a fit of giggles, quickly smothered as her mother turned a wrathful eye on her. Indeed she all but cowered against her father. Olivia felt an instinctive flare of protectiveness. So Georgina wasn't the apple of her mother's eye, then! How very sad! Thinking that, she held out a hand to the child, much as she had done all her life with her younger sisters. "So, Georgina!"

It was done so naturally, McAlpine thought with a rush of gratitude. Indeed beautifully. She hadn't a thought in her head that her gesture would be refused.

"It's down to you and me," she was saying, smiling down at his daughter. "I thought you might like the Persian room? At least, I'm calling it the Persian room."

"You mean the one with the dome and the doors?" Georgina looked mightily surprised.

"The very one," Olivia confirmed. Surely Georgina hadn't been expecting to be relegated to the old nursery. Always supposing there was one.

"Oh, goody!" Georgina surprised everyone, including herself, by holding tight to Olivia's hand "You know what it means." She fastened her eyes on Olivia's serenely beautiful face. "It means I'm really grown up."

"Of course you are." Olivia gave the small hand in hers a reassuring squeeze.

Bessie came to her door with a beautiful, brilliantly coloured parrot sitting happily on her shoulder.

"Oh, there you are! Come in." Olivia was setting out a choice of evening dresses on the bed.

"Don't worry. He ain't stayin'." Bessie went to the open doors that led onto the garden, sending her feathered friend on his way. Bessie had no task for the evening. As a tribal princess she wasn't expected to wait at table. Bessie's job was to offer guidance in any number of capacities.

"So take a look," Olivia invited, more at home in Bessie's company with every passing day.

"Let's see now!" Bessie carefully examined all three dresses, staying quiet as she did it. Olivia had chosen her "best black" despite McAlpine's scoffing, a pair of silk-satin evening trousers—trousers suited her—in a deep amethyst that had a matching bloused top and, lastly, a sapphire-blue two-piece outfit that she thought was maybe a little overkill for tonight. After all, she was a girl who had spent her life trying to deflect attention from herself.

The third outfit consisted of a long skirt, and a camisole top that hung from shoestring straps. There was a wide sash to match. It looked very nice on her but the cami was a bit on the bare side. She really should have had the straps shortened so the vee didn't dip into her cleavage. Not that there was that much of it. But enough. How many times had Bella told her she was jeopardising all her chances? What, by giving peeks of her breasts to potential admirers? Bella was the Lorelei. Not a role that suited Olivia.

"Why don't we have a little fun?" Bessie suggested. She began to sing something that sounded like an advertising jingle and, in fact, was. "This goes with this and that goes with this…" As she sang, she began switching the two-piece outfits around on the bed. "You wanna look your best?" She shot a questioning glance at Olivia.

"I don't want to put Mrs McAlpine's pretty nose out of joint," Olivia said wryly. "I'm the hired help."

"What did yah think of her?" Bessie snorted like a brumby.

"Yes, well…"

"She don't bring the best outta people," Bessie said sagely. "Now, Livvy, there are two ways to go. My way. And your way. I can't ever get to wear things like this in me whole life, but I *know*. I know colour. I say the amethyst evenin' pants paired with the Ulysses-butterfly-blue top. Show off yah beautiful eyes. Yah got such a narrow waist…make a big bow with the sash."

Olivia stood quietly considering. "Right-o, Bessie," she said finally, tapping Bessie lightly on the shoulder. "I'm happy to go your way. I trust you."

"Trust very important in life," said Bessie. "By the way, got something for yah." She dipped a hand into the voluminous pocket of her hand-painted skirt. "To you it's a charm. To me it's magic handed down from the Ancients. It'll protect yah, my lovely Pommy friend."

"From what, Bessie?" Olivia felt a tiny shiver of alarm. "Do you think I need protecting?"

"Jus' to be on the safe side," Bessie answered mildly, handing Olivia a highly polished oval stone, some two inches in length and almost as wide. It was flashing exquisite iridescent colours that included blue, blue-green, violet-blue and amethyst. Someone had set the piece in a silver bezel with a silver chain fixed to the back, so it could be worn as a necklace.

"But, Bessie, this is beautiful!" Olivia began to examine the crystal in detail. Obviously it had a spiritual quality for Bessie. She thought she felt some of it herself as she stroked the crystal with her forefinger.

"Come on. Show me. Put it on." Bessie combined gentleness with what Olivia now recognised as inherent authority.

"Heavens, Bessie, you sound really worried."

"Don't want no one messing yah up," said Bessie, standing back to scrutinise the effect. "That's exactly right. Knew it would. Help yah go towards the light. Think of it as a spiritual guide. Touch it often."

"But surely you want it back, Bessie." Olivia was near moved to tears by Bessie's caring and concern. "It must mean a lot to you."

"I give it to you. Our paths cross for a reason, Livvy. Never doubt it."

Olivia was beginning to think Bessie was right. She felt a mad urge to ask Bessie to arrange a magic spell so McAlpine would fall in love with her. She didn't have the slightest doubt Bessie could.

* * *

Bessie wasn't her only visitor. Georgina came to her room just as Olivia was planning on checking on the child to see if she was happy and had everything she needed. It had been a considerable coup choosing the Persian room, something she would have adored herself at Georgina's age, for Georgina had shown great excitement at being allowed to occupy the room she saw "fit for an Arabian princess." It had a remarkable domed ceiling, a mosaic of brilliant colours, wooden shutter doors carved with the Islamic-star grid, a very beautiful antique Persian rug, a huge four-poster bed and soft furnishings in a kaleidoscope of colours.

Of course, Olivia had checked with McAlpine when he was working in his study, which would have found favour with his father. It was so much the gentleman's club in style and furnishings, it really demanded a dress code. He had lifted his dark auburn head as she entered, albeit with that big-cat gleam in his eyes. She'd had another daydream about him lately...*pouncing...* *licking her all over...*

"Now this is a pleasant surprise!" He closed a thick file and set it aside. "What can I do for you, Olivia? Race it by me. Not a lot of time." He beckoned her to lose herself in one of the man-size leather armchairs.

"I propose putting Georgina into a different room," she told him as though not expecting to encounter opposition. Neatly she crossed her slender legs at the ankle.

"Her usual bedroom not good enough?"

"It's very nice," she conceded graciously. "But at twelve years of age she would have outgrown it."

He sat back, locking his two hands behind his head. "Marigole herself did the designing."

"I guessed that. Your ex-wife is a woman of considerable style. Bu she would have designed it with her little girl in mind. Time passes. Georgina is now a young lady."

"So what exactly have you got in mind?"

"I thought the Persian room. At least, that's what I call it."

Amusement bracketed his mouth. "That was my mother's plan."

"Really?" Her face turned incandescent. "I'd so like to meet your mother."

"And it may well come to that, Ms Balfour. The Persian room, you say!" He took a moment considering. "Who am I to go against you? The room is strewn with valuable antiques. I'm sure you noticed, just as I'm sure you were used to a whole lot grander as a child."

"You're concerned your daughter might damage them?" She lifted delicately arched brows several shades darker than her hair.

"Well, she has been tossing a few things around of late, but everything can be replaced. My daughter can't. As long as she's happy there, that's all that matters. I would have thought, myself, it was a bit overwhelming for a youngster."

"Trust me. As you say, I've slept amid grandeur." Olivia spoke entirely without pretension. That was the way her life was. "I'm sure your daughter is a highly intelligent, thinking child. If for some reason she doesn't want to be there, I can make alternative arrangements. Her usual room needs to be done over from scratch. Georgina is ready to move on."

McAlpine threw up his hands in feigned dismay. "If only you hadn't mentioned moving on, Ms Balfour," he cried. "I must tell you, I dread to lose you."

If only that were true!

"Everything OK, Georgy?" Georgina, far from being difficult as Olivia had feared, was acting like a well-brought-up young girl, requesting Olivia call her by her nickname. "I was just coming along to see if you were happy."

"Oh, I am! I love the room you've given me. I love what you've done with the flowers." Georgina was dressed in a pretty white nightgown with a matching robe, her long hair brushed to a high sheen. "You're really nice, aren't you?"

"Absolutely!" Olivia smiled at her. "I have seven sisters, you know. All younger than me. That means I got the role of big sister."

"I bet you're a lovely sister. Very kind."

"I try to be, Georgy. Do please sit down. What do you think of my outfit?" The child had begun studying Olivia like a dresser trained to give a very difficult mistress just the comment required. "Bessie helped me with it."

"Bessie?" Georgy's silky eyebrows shot up. "Was she here?"

"About an hour ago. I have great faith in Bessie's sense of colour."

"You're honoured," Georgy said sincerely. "Did Bessie give you that sparkling necklace? It's some sort of crystal, isn't it? It's sending out coloured rays. Most probably, it's magic. It looks *amazing*! Better than diamonds. Anyone can have diamonds. Bessie is a princess in her own tribe. Her real name is Eerina."

"But that's lovely." Olivia looked up. "It suits her much better than Bessie."

"I know. One of the elders in her family was a kurdaitcha man. Do you know what that means?"

"Sorcerer?" Olivia took an educated guess.

Georgy nodded, impressed. "They're invisible to their enemies. They wear special slippers made out of emu feathers. The kurdaitcha man is very powerful. He's like James Bond. He's licensed to kill."

"Good grief!" Olivia mimed a freak-out.

"A sorcerer can sing a man to death," Georgy continued, thrilled with her captive audience. "He can send his spirit form anywhere in a whirlwind. They know all about magic. So does Bessie, but she won't let on."

"Good thing we're her friends," Olivia commented, enjoying the sound of Georgy's silvery peal of laughter. "So what's your verdict on my outfit? It was Bessie's idea to mix and match."

The brightness drained out of Georgy's face. "Mummy is going to be very jealous," she warned. "Are you Daddy's girlfriend?"

She should be so lucky! "Lord, no! It's just as your father said. I'm here on a study tour."

"But everything about you says you're rich!"

"My *father* is rich, Georgy." Olivia didn't mention her healthy trust fund. "I haven't had a real job up to date. Listen, can you keep a secret?" Suddenly she wanted to be truthful with the child.

"A secret?" Georgy's huge eyes turned to saucers.

"Trust is important. I trust *you*, Georgy." Trust made vulnerable people feel stronger she had found.

Georgy looked greatly heartened. "Are you *going* to be Daddy's girlfriend?" She sounded as if she didn't mind.

She hoped Georgy wouldn't notice her flush. "No, nothing like that. I did something that greatly upset my father. So I'm rather on the outer. My father wanted me out of the country for a while. Lying low, I suppose you'd call it."

"I can't believe *you* would make such a mistake. You look like you've never made a mistake in your whole life."

"That's only at first glance. I'm not nearly as sure of myself as I might appear. I'm two people really."

"Oh, yes, I *know*!" Georgy began to rock herself back and forth. "So am I. There's the person you want to be and the person you're supposed to be."

"Exactly. I knew you'd understand perfectly. So now you know my secret. I'm here to pull up my socks and do better. That was the challenge my father handed down."

"He doesn't sound like a pleasant man, your father?" Georgy advanced an opinion.

"He's a very important man. A man of consequence. The head of a dynasty. It makes for being prideful, controlling. Much is expected of him. He expects much of us. Me, in particular, because I'm the eldest."

"So what did you *do*?" Georgy cast around in her mind for a social disaster. "Did you fall down drunk at a nightclub?"

"Never got round to *that* one, Georgy. I'm a staid person, really. But I have a twin, Bella. We love each other dearly. We rarely have words. But one night at a big gala ball we got into a fight. Wrong time, wrong place. Sadly we were overheard by a journalist who managed to get it on to the front page of his newspaper. My father is a proud man from an old illustrious family. He doesn't take kindly to being publicly humiliated."

"But that doesn't make sense!" Georgy was clearly on Olivia's side. "You and Bella had a fight. Was it a catfight? Can't imagine it with you. Were you pulling each other's hair out, swearing, saying four-letter words?"

"Dear heaven, no!" Olivia shuddered. "But it was a family matter that should never have seen the light of day."

"Rather like Daddy and Mummy's divorce," Georgy said sadly. "There was a lot about it in the newspapers. I hated it. All the kids knew. Mummy actually told a newsreader she was going to take Daddy for all he was worth. Isn't that disgusting? One kid said he had too much anyway. Mummy said things about him I knew weren't true. I love Daddy best in the whole world. My mother doesn't need me or want me. She doesn't like the way I'm twelve, nearly thirteen, and she's thirty-eight. She *hates* getting older. I must remind her of what she used to look like. You'd think Mummy's sort of woman would want a daughter. The girly-girly thing. But she doesn't want me. She said if she had given Daddy a son the marriage would never have broken up."

Dear heaven, fancy laying that on a child! Olivia was appalled. "Do you believe that, Georgy?" She gave thanks her father had never bemoaned the fact he didn't have a son. Being her father he might yet get around to fathering one. Her father wasn't cured of beautiful women by a long shot.

Georgy turned sad eyes on Olivia. "I don't know what to believe. Why should she say such a thing?"

One possible answer was she was terribly callous. "But you asked your father?"

"Daddy always says the same thing. He *adores* me. He wouldn't change me for anyone else in the world."

Good for him!

"Well, then!" Olivia spoke bracingly. "You must believe exactly that."

"But I still know I'm part of the problem," Georgy mourned. "I've always loved Daddy best ever since I can remember. I don't think my mother *cares*, Olivia." She looked earnestly into Olivia's concerned face. "She doesn't. Daddy can have full custody. That's why I'm here. She likes to pretend she's not abandoning me, but she is. She knows Daddy will always love and care for me. That lets her off the hook. A lot of kids at school live with divorce. Usually it's the dad that takes off with someone. That happened to two of my friends. I know my dad would never abandon me. But he's an important man like your father. He doesn't have a lot of *time*."

But he is making time for his daughter.

That scored him a lot of points.

She met up with McAlpine as she was making her way along the vaulted corridor. It was hung with an astounding collection of paintings of the Red Centre. Once she would have thought the colours glorified, but now she knew better. She had actually seen these dry pottery colours—the pinks, the yellows, the rust red of the earth, the grape blue and the amethyst of the distant escarpments, the cobalt blue of the sky.

"Well, well!" He came to a dead stop as he accepted an undeniable truth. He wanted this woman. Yet he continued to play the suave bantering game. "May I say how absolutely stunning you look, Ms Balfour. Not that I didn't know you could dazzle. The outfit is a master stroke." His golden eyes assessed her from head to toe.

Much as a great couturier would inspect his favourite muse, Olivia thought. At least he *really* liked what he saw. She registered that from the flash in his eyes. It gave her enormous confidence. She wasn't in any way nervous of this evening or his guests. Apart from the sometime she-devil, Marigole, who mightn't be able to resist getting in a dig or two.

"And the goddess hair!" He headed towards her. "I believe there are dangers inherent in falling in love with a goddess."

"Mockery, McAlpine?" She turned assessing blue eyes on him. He was wearing evening dress. He looked magnificent. Black tailored trousers, black collarless shirt, a midnight-blue tailored jacket over the top. It was a very sophisticated look and quite a change from black tie.

"Indeed, no. How modest you are. You have marvellous hair."

"And it's all mine." She couldn't help laughing. "No need of extensions, though you probably don't know much about that." Her voice was surprisingly steady when she felt sexual excitement working its way down from her throat through her centre to her legs. Bella had described him as "one sexy devil!" Bella was never wrong.

"I'm not that far behind the times," he said, thrilling her by taking her arm as if they were paired for the night. "For a while I puzzled over how a lady friend of mine grew an impressive mane overnight."

"So you're telling me you have lady friends?"

"Don't be ridiculous, Olivia." He glanced down at her, inhaling her subtle exquisite perfume. "You make it sound like a crime. I could have a whole harem if I wanted it."

"No doubt!" She broke off, aware her heart was banging away like a set of drums. His golden eyes were fixed on her cleavage which didn't seem terribly like him. There was nothing vaguely lecherous about McAlpine for all his sexual magnetism. "What are you looking at?" she asked unsteadily.

"The necklace," he told her with the tiniest frown. "Bessie gave it to you?"

She clutched the glittering, glowing stone. "Bessie, yes. That's a relief. I thought you were staring at my cleavage."

"That too," he purred, narrowing his golden eyes.

Heat enveloped her. "Bessie actually chose what I've got on, the top of one outfit and the evening trousers of another."

"And she got it exactly right. Bessie has a great eye for colour."

"Georgy insisted I leave my hair loose. I've been outnumbered on that score since I arrived. I'm honoured Bessie gave me this necklace. She said it's a talisman."

"To protect you from all harm." He was well aware of the significance of the iridescent stone. "I'm glad you feel honoured, Olivia, You *are*. Bessie, Princess Eerina, outranks you."

She surprised him by showing him a lovely, spontaneous smile. Her blue eyes danced. Her beautiful mouth curved. He was aware of the barriers she had built up through the years and fought hard to keep in place. Time they fell. Entirely.

"I had that feeling about Bessie from the moment I met her. It's beautiful, the stone, isn't it? So unusual."

It looked magical, sitting perfectly between her creamy breasts, inviting a man's worshipping hands. *His*, if he was going to admit to it. She was showing more of those high creamy breasts than usual. Not a lot. Just enough. Nevertheless his mouth went dry. Her appearance was wreaking havoc with his senses. He, McAlpine, who could have any number of willing women, had to get a grip. "It throws out a different light with your every movement." He gave a nod of approval when he wanted desperately to be alone with her and hang all his guests. He couldn't even prevent a sigh. "I suppose we shouldn't linger. Our guests will be waiting."

"*Your* guests," she pointed out, trying to control a flush.

"You *are* the hostess."

"Well, I hope I make you proud," she murmured huskily, aware beneath the smooth layers of banter he was finding her as desirable as she found him.

CHAPTER SEVEN

PREDINNER drinks, then on to dinner.

Olivia willed herself to calm as Marigole broke away from the group to hurry towards her as though Olivia was her latest best friend. She had taken a minute to check on the kitchen. All in order, just as she knew it would be. Kath and the girls had given her the thumbs up.

"You're a star!" Kath, the spokeswoman, had delivered the unanimous verdict.

But it was the golden flare in McAlpine's eyes that had put her on cloud nine. She'd even caught a flicker of surprise in the knockout Chloe's eyes. Didn't think she had it in her? Well, she hadn't until Bessie had stepped in as fashion guru.

In the end it was Marigole who wore the little black dress, a saucy number if ever there was one—very short to show off her dancer's legs, the neckline curving in low. Killer black evening sandals with strapping adorned her small feet; radiant silver lustred pearls dropped in a shepherd's hook hung from her ears. Olivia was impressed. Marigole was a very glamorous woman and she could obviously afford the best.

And, surprises for everyone—who obviously went back years with Marigole—she had greeted Olivia affably, complimenting her on her outfit and what great hair she had. "You can't know how many times I've cried into my pillow about mine," she exclaimed, waiting a second or two for someone to offer amazement. They didn't. "Ever since I had Georgina it simply won't *grow*."

"The bob suits you beautifully," Olivia said. It was no less than the truth.

"And it comes at a price!" Marigole tossed off a laugh. "I have to say I'm taken aback by the thing you have around your neck! A bit tacky, dear! Then I suppose you didn't bring any of your jewellery with you?"

"Strange if I did." Olivia had been prepared in advance for Marigole to bare her true self. As an insult, it didn't carry a lot of sting. "I'll only be here for a short time. I don't share your opinion of the necklace. I think it's beautiful."

Marigole half cupped her hand around her mouth as though fearing she would be overheard. "My dear, it's just a piece of junk you can pick up at street markets."

Although the smile was bright, smile and tone didn't match up. There was something vaguely threatening about Marigole's demeanour, causing Olivia to do as Bessie had instructed—gently rub her flashing magic crystal.

Even afterwards she wasn't sure what happened. Had she imagined it? A trick of the light? All she did know was a ripple of apprehension ran down her back. Pinpoints of blue light had manifested themselves in Marigole's dark eyes like some weird phenomenon.

"God!" Marigole suddenly screeched. "What the hell are you doing?"

"Doing?" For the life of her Olivia couldn't clear up that mystery. She watched transfixed as Marigole threw out her arm as if stung by a wasp. At the precise moment McAlpine swiftly closed in on them, alerted by his ex-wife's all-too-familiar screech. He had been carrying a crystal flute of champagne, but the flailing of Marigole's arm knocked the flute clean out of his hand. Sparkling wine flew out of the flute, splashing onto the carpet, giving Marigole a good spray on the way down.

"OK, so it's *not* Krug." McAlpine tried to make a joke of it but his ex-wife wasn't having any.

"She shone something in my eyes," Marigole erupted, to all appearances in dead earnest.

"You're seriously asking me to believe that?" McAlpine looked at Olivia as if in apology. "Do not make a scene, Marigole," he stressed.

"Let me get you a napkin." Olivia, innocent of any wrongdoing, was feeling positively guilty. "I don't think the wine did any lasting damage to your beautiful dress. I'll get someone to mop the wine from the carpet."

"And how would you know about the damage to my dress?" Marigole's petite body was coiled in fury. "It cost a fortune. I'm appalled. You shone a light in my eyes. Enough to blind me."

"As in some high-powered ray?" McAlpine's expression was caustic. "Though where Olivia could be hiding it, I can't imagine." As he spoke he produced a snowy-white handkerchief, handing it to his ex-wife. "She can't have shoved it down her camisole."

Olivia took a deep breath. "Marigole, I did nothing but watch you throw out your arm. I thought something had stung you."

"Then where's the mark?" Marigole cried, holding up her right, then her left, arm for inspection. "What's that?" Marigole couldn't hold back her disbelief.

"I'd call *that* a bite," McAlpine said, his voice a dark rumble. A red welt about the size of a five-cent piece had appeared on Marigole's right arm. "You need to put something on it." He wondered how any stinging insect had got into a room like this.

"I'll get it." Olivia turned away at once. She would have to put what she *thought* she saw out of her mind. It was a trick of the light. Nothing else. But the red welt made no sense at all. She'd had Marigole under close observation the entire time. There had been no red welt on her arm. It had only appeared when Marigole had demanded to know where the mark was.

Maybe there's some ancient curse attached to the stone?
Don't be silly!
The aboriginal people are much concerned with magic.
I'm not listening.
At least think about it.

* * *

By the time the main course was out of the way and dessert was being served by Kathy's well-trained girls, Marigole had regained her equilibrium. Even more extraordinary to Olivia's eyes was the fact the red welt had entirely disappeared. Was the local snake oil as effective as all that? She should order in a couple of bottles.

Much to her satisfaction, each course had been received with enthusiasm.

McAlpine caught her eye, raised his wineglass in a silent toast to her. He saw with pleasure how the lovely colour warmed her cheeks. Tonight she was as beautiful and serene as a swan. Breeding showed. She would make some man a splendid wife. He could have mourned the fact he hadn't met a woman like her years ago, but then he reminded himself she would have been a student at Oxford. Just a girl. Selfless, devoted, overseeing too much for a demanding father. Not that Oscar wasn't very proud of her. But Oscar had shaped the life his daughter was now finding she wanted to be free of. He didn't fool himself that a woman like Olivia Balfour could settle in a desert kingdom, though his business affairs took him all over the world. He would want a clever woman like Olivia at his side. He was long past wanting an affair. He wanted *her*. Heart, mind and body. Only wanting and getting were two different things.

Marigole, unlike the others, wasn't so much eating and enjoying the various dishes as rearranging what was presented to her into a more pleasing pattern on her plate. Either way she didn't take more than a bite, demonstrating her awesome self-discipline. A very different story, however, with the wines. His ex-wife obviously rejected the theory that one to two small glasses of wine a day was enough for a woman as classic scare tactics from the medical profession. He genuinely wished Marigole well. But he wanted her out of his life. She had done enough damage. It was Georgina who had to be considered.

The conversation ranged easily and fluently over a broad number of topics, touching on the political and also, of great interest to Olivia, dressage, or as it was often referred to, "horse ballet."

Olivia herself had been an upper-level dressage competitor in her early twenties.

"Babs is a wonderful equestrienne," Barbara Corbett's husband said proudly, no mean horseman himself, having come second to his friend, McAlpine, in several top-notch cross-country endurance races.

Everyone at the table was a seasoned world traveller which provided an additional source of discussion. McAlpine and his friend Brendan juggled the conversational balls back and forth between them. Both were charming, witty and clever. It was McAlpine who started talking about the adventures they had shared since boyhood. And there were many, including an unforgettable trip to Antarctica.

"But if you want to know how the world began, you might try visiting the Galapagos Islands," McAlpine said. "Bren and I once watched a volcano erupting from the deck of a yacht we'd chartered."

"I do hope at a safe distance," Olivia offered to general laughter.

"Safe enough." McAlpine winged a smile in her direction. "You should have been there, Olivia, to hear the way the lava roared and hissed as it poured into the cold current. The violence of it, the shooting flames of molten red in the darkness! God, it was exciting! It's volcanos like that and the others that make up the archipelago where Darwin cracked his code of evolution."

Brendan picked up on that to add the disturbing news that the giant Galapagos tortoises were being senselessly slaughtered by pirates on floating fish factories.

"Oh, for God's sake, don't let's talk about tortoises," Marigole interrupted with great impatience, much put out by the way the superposh Balfour woman managed to shine throughout the evening. Worse, her ex-husband's gleaming eyes were alighting on her far too frequently. "Save the whales, save the trees, save the tortoises! How boring! You weren't being entirely truthful telling us you were here on a study tour were you, Olivia?" she accused, a teeny slurring to her words.

Lucas, who had been thoroughly enjoying himself, suddenly looked perturbed. His neck, half covered by an expensive silk cravat, went a deep red. It was apparent to all of them he was seriously worried about what Marigole was about to say.

None more so than McAlpine, who had survived his marriage for a relatively long period. "You have a great nose for gossip, haven't you, Marigole? I'm sure, in this case, none of us wants to hear it. Certainly not Lucas, who is looking alarmed."

More like freaked out! Olivia thought, strongly suspecting what was to come next. Her stomach muscles clenched in anticipation of an attack.

"My dear chap—" Lucas addressed McAlpine directly, apparently desperate not to be part of anything Marigole might say.

But Marigole, not to be denied her moment of triumph, cut in. "As I hear it, you were banished for bad behaviour." The *B*s were given full explosive throttle.

"If that's the case, I'll say a prayer for you, Olivia." Brendan yawned, as if uninterested in anything Marigole might say.

But Olivia wasn't her father's daughter for nothing. "Not the sentence I would have applied myself, Marigole," she said, not losing her cool composure. "My father simply wanted his daughters out of the spotlight for a time. I'm certain there's nothing unusual about that? Obviously you've been doing some checking. One wonders why?"

"Blue Blood Turns Bad!" Again the *B*s shot out like bullets. It was obvious Marigole had no thought whatever for anyone's feelings. "Wasn't that the way the headlines ran? The high-and-mighty Balfours and their illicit affairs! Not one but *two* illegitimate daughters! I'm shocked. I don't know if I want my daughter near you."

It was Brendan who blew his top. He had worn best-man regalia for his closest friend and ever after wished he had expressed his heartfelt doubts about Marigole long before the event. "Marigole, what a vicious bitch you are!" There was a fierce scowl on his face. "What you really need—"

"Is an early night." McAlpine held up an authoritative hand to indicate his friend should stop there.

Red flags mounted to Marigole's cheeks. "And who do you think you are? You're not *God,* Clint."

"How would you know? You don't speak to Him."

Marigole was not to be deflected. "Why is this woman here?" She was displaying all the bitterness and sense of betrayal appropriate in a wife. "Are you sleeping with her?"

Brendan's current girlfriend, Chloe, who wasn't exactly renowned for her IQ, uttered a shocked four-letter word beneath her breath. She thought the ex–Mrs McAlpine, though still a stunner at thirty-eight, should keep well clear of the booze.

McAlpine gave them a taste of the dominant male. He slammed a fist onto the table. "That's quite enough. Olivia is a guest in my home."

"And I've been sleeping very soundly at night, Mrs McAlpine," Olivia assured her. "Alone. Does that answer your question? Not that I can see it's your business."

"Damned right!" Brendan gave Olivia a look of stout support.

Only Marigole was staring back at Olivia, apparently oblivious to anyone else. "I'm serious."

"So am I." Olivia was debating whether to call on her magic crystal again. She had an urge to touch it but backed off in case it knocked Marigole clean out of her chair.

Her man of the moment, Lucas, wore the deep remorseful expression of a basset hound. One could only marvel at the contrast between McAlpine and his successor! "I'm so sorry, Olivia. I'm afraid in an unguarded moment—"

"Lucas, if you would escort Marigole to her room," McAlpine asked suavely, "before she nods off?"

A bitter laugh from Marigole. "What a beast you are, Clint! I'm not a child to be sent from the table."

"Off you go." He waved a hand. "We'll see you at breakfast perhaps."

* * *

Such an embarrassing incident should have put paid to the success of the evening. With Marigole out of the way no such thing happened. They all adjourned to the great room for coffee and liqueurs, the subject of Olivia's "banishment" dropped as if no one knew or cared what Marigole had been talking about. Alternatively they *did* know but didn't consider it a big deal in the light of daily catastrophes and revealed illegitimacies. Even among the high and mighty. Lucas, however, did not return. Very possibly a lover's tiff? Marigole would have seized on her new target with renewed vigour. It would have been obvious to a blind man—why not Lucas?—that Marigole was still deeply in thrall to her ex-husband. Love or hate? Lucas, nice as he was, could never in his life have inspired either. And he had been married twice.

The evening finally came to an end well after midnight with everyone deciding to meet up for breakfast around 8:30 a.m. A swim in a safe freshwater lagoon? Not for me, thought Olivia, feeling her stomach lurch. And who could blame her? The odd saltwater monster had found its way into a few peaceful havens. She didn't know then that someone in the party always carried a rifle. Just in case.

Maybe take the horses out? More to her liking. All were accomplished riders, except Brendan's girlfriend, Chloe, who claimed she didn't know one end of a horse from the other.

"Then I shall teach you, little darling," promised Brendan.

Everyone had retired when Olivia suddenly remembered she had left her crystal necklace on a table in the great room. She had taken it off so Barbara, who was fascinated by it, could examine the stone more closely. She had meant to put it back on, but had become distracted by a question from Chloe about life in London. She wasn't anxious about the necklace. No one would touch it. Nevertheless she felt the urge to go get it as though she should always keep it by her side. The huge house was softly aglow. The main lights had been switched off, leaving on soft downlights. No guest would be called on to wander about in darkness.

She had discovered she loved this house. Although she had lived all her life in a grand country house—very large, very dark, very old—much as she loved Balfour Manor and its great park, the house with its enormous panelled rooms and endless corridors could at times be oppressive. It was also crowded to the hilt with valuable furniture, paintings, tapestries, marbles and porcelains, dating back centuries, to say nothing of a couple of resident ghosts. Everywhere one looked at the manor, there were so many splendid things to behold it was near impossible to focus on any one object. Growing up as she had she had become quite a connoisseur of art and could speak very knowledgeably about it. So it came as something of a shock to realise, though born a Balfour, she could easily and happily move into this extraordinary house in its even more extraordinary Northern Territory setting. There were beautiful and valuable things here as well, but there was no danger of bumping into anything. And the *air*! The pure golden air, the quality of the sunlight, the colorations of the vast empty landscape! It was like living inside an Albert Namatjira painting.

She had lived a life of privilege, but it had its downside in constriction, relentless media attention, living up to her father's very exacting standards. Really, she'd had none of the freedom she found here. She didn't want to be disloyal but it was as if she'd been handed a get-out-of-jail-free card. And to think in a few months' time she would have to pack up again and go away!

Doesn't bear thinking about.

She was passing McAlpine's study, necklace in hand, when the brass knob on the door turned. She jumped like a startled cat.

"Olivia!" He stood there, the most dashingly romantic-looking man in the world, delivering her name on a slow-drawn breath. "Were you about to knock on my door? Could I be so lucky! How did you know I was still up?"

Her heart started up its now-familiar thumping routine. For a moment she was too off balance to smile or even speak. "I haven't been keeping tabs on you, if that's what you mean. I left my necklace in the great room. I'd been showing it to Barbara. I thought I should come and get it, seeing as it's my very special talisman."

"It might very well be," he said in a deepening tone. "You're not going to sleep in it, are you?"

"Under my pillow," she said. No wonder she was fighting to keep calm. He looked shockingly sexy, on high alert, very elegant but dangerous. He had taken off his jacket and slipped a couple of buttons on his black silk shirt for extra comfort. His skin, she saw, beyond the light mat of hair was like polished bronze.

"So what happened tonight?" he asked. "The stone arranged it?"

She was held by the force of those golden eyes. "Why ever would you say that? Marigole was stung. Wasn't she?"

"She was stung all right, but not by any flying insect I know of. Do show me that stone again if you would."

She opened out her palm.

"See. It's duller and darker."

Her head bent nearer his, golden blonde, a wonderful foil for rich dark auburn. "So?" She stared up at him perplexed. "Has it lost its powers?"

He gave a brief laugh. "I see we're both in agreement it *has* powers."

"Well, I'm not going to say it hasn't and be struck dead."

"Me either. I've seen too many extraordinary things in my time, all to do with aboriginal sorcery and magic. Your stone is governed by kinetic forces, movement, being close to your heart. Put it back on for a while."

"Are you serious?"

"Why are you whispering?" he asked gently.

"I don't know." She was, in fact, caught up in high tension.

"Here, let me. If you'll just grab that glorious mane and hold it out of the way."

At the touch of his hands on her nape she felt her blood glitter. Her father would have frowned at her "glamour girl" look. The wrong look, he considered, for her. "I've been so accustomed to pulling my hair back," she said shakily. "I don't feel like myself with it floating around."

"Your *old* self," he stressed. "I love it! It's the new you! Now turn around."

She would when she could steady herself.

"OK, I'll turn you." His hands slid to her shoulders. "There! Your magic talisman has come alive again."

Her eyes dipped to her breast. The sparkle had returned, along with the flash of iridescent colours. "I suspected Eerina was a sorceress the minute I met her. How does one get to be like that?" She lifted her eyes to meet his, felt a swift pulsing of sexual desire.

"You're a sorceress in your own way," he said, his tone low. "Right now I feel quite powerless."

"*You*, powerless? To do what?" She was still whispering, trying to pull herself out of an erotic trance.

"Resist you," he said. Dead serious. No flirtation.

He stood there, looking at her with such intensity that she felt herself swaying towards him. They were only a breath away.

You've found him! But what about the highly antagonistic ex-wife, Georgy's mother?

"I should go," she said falteringly.

"Don't." He caught the silky flesh of her arm, turned it, exposing her narrow wrist with its fine tracery of blue veins. While she held her constricted breath, he slowly raised her upturned hand to his mouth. "If I start anything more, I won't stop," he confessed. His voice sounded torched. Maybe tormented. Gently he touched his mouth to her wrist, his tongue a warm pulse on the blue veins. "I want you. You know that?" He lifted his head, casting aside all pretence.

Olivia felt a blinding rush of something beyond pleasure. All serenity had left her. She was adrift on a wild sea. She tried to explain. "This level of feeling is frightening to me, Clint. I've led such a quiet, contained life. No impressive collection of lovers. So please don't lead me on if you don't mean it. I couldn't bear to be another victim."

"Victim? I don't lie." The denial came out on a harsh rasp. He was still holding her hand, his thumb rubbing back and forth over her transparent wrist. "The truth is, I want you more and more every day. I acknowledge there's terror in that. For both of us."

"You fear to put yourself in a woman's hands again?"

His stunning features had drawn taut with desire. "You could be the one exception. I want to scoop you up and take you to my bed."

"But that doesn't answer the question. We're drawn to each other. We were from the beginning, I think, even though your way with me was infuriating."

"I realise now I was spectacularly rude."

"You were," she said raggedly.

"Forgive me?" His smile was slow and heart melting. "Kiss and make up?"

Oh, God, yes!

She had been waiting for him all her life. Here was one man who wouldn't let her hide away. Voluptuously she let her head fall back. Her eyes closed. Her senses were reeling. Rapture was flooding her brain and her body. That intense longing manifested itself in a sob that was muffled beneath the weight of his mouth.

She would never forget being kissed like this. Not if she lived until she was one hundred. The erotic splendour of it all drew her into its glory. No matter what happened—she was far from certain of what lay ahead of them—she would remember these moments out of time.

Involuntary tears rose to her eyes. An ache of yearning and anguish.

"Olivia?" He drew back, a sharp catch of concern in his voice. "Surely I'm not making you cry?"

"Women cry when they need to."

Her tone stabbed at his heart. Was he rushing her, frightening her with the strength of his ardour? "Olivia, I'm here to take good care of you. You're under my protection. I'm sorry if I'm moving too fast. I have to remember I'm older than you and far more experienced. I must apologise too if Marigole upset you tonight."

"She did upset me," Olivia admitted, drawing back very slightly. "The malice behind it! I'm rather good at hiding my upsets."

"I know. But there's nothing much I can do about Marigole," he told her tersely. "She's a tease and a bully, but she's also Georgy's mother. Sometimes I think I'll always have Marigole in my life."

"Because of the daughter you created together?" She spoke with the utmost gravity, mindful of that fact.

"Well, yes."

"I understand." She did. "But surely when you remarry?"

His golden eyes burned into her. "It has to be the right woman. Marriage can bring out the best in people and the worst. Only an idiot would make the same mistake twice."

"So you're not ready for commitment?"

He knit his dark brows together. It gave him a dangerous air. "Are you?" He badly needed to know.

She looked away towards a painting. Not really seeing it. "I want to get married. I want children. I love children. But, like you, I'm frightened of making a mess of my life, settling on the wrong man."

"You want a *safe* man?"

She gave a broken little laugh, more like a sob. "When I first saw you coming towards me at the airport, I thought, *My God, a wild man!*"

His expression lightened. "I'm sure I looked like one after Justin."

"Justin told me he was very fond of me."

"God!" he exclaimed in disgust. "Couldn't he do better than that?"

"Seems not!" She shrugged her creamy shoulders. "I suppose I've always appeared sort of ordinary beside Bella. Half the eligible men we knew were in love with her. And used me to get to her."

"More accessible," he said. "Bella is very beautiful and vivacious. I rather formed the impression Oscar enjoyed Bella's wildness. She could get away with things you couldn't. Ever think you proved too difficult? Too unassailable? That touch-me-not air. I like it. What I like better is touching you. But as I pointed out once before, there are inherent dangers in falling at a goddess's feet."

The way he was looking at her—surely with a marvellous tenderness—made her want to sob her heart out. Get rid of the pain. The pain of years of conforming to what her father wanted. He was right. As always. Their father *had* enjoyed Bella's escapades, barring the last one. Bella was allowed to go wild. It was condoned. Olivia had been obliged to toe the line. A lone tear like a crystal drop trickled down her cheek.

"Olivia! Come here to me." His mastery of her was running at full throttle. He drew her back into his arms, cradling her against his chest. It was extraordinary the way he made her feel small and deeply feminine. As much a woman as she could ever be.

She let him cradle her, revelling in his strength. "Don't mind me," she murmured. "I'm ashamed of myself really for breaking down like this."

"But I *do* mind you," he said tautly. "I thought we'd established that. For all your sophistication, your age, your beauty, you still carry around the grave child you once were. Lift your head."

She was compelled to obey, driven by desire. His head bent over hers, the tip of his tongue catching up the teardrop that still lay on her cheek, taking it into his mouth. "I can't waste one of your tears. Don't let me frighten you away, Olivia. Sometimes I think of you as a gorgeous butterfly that's alighted on my shoulder. One false move and you'll fly off!"

"Clint!" Her voice broke with helpless emotion.

"I've never heard my name sound so good!" He dropped an exquisitely gentle kiss on her mouth. It pierced her with such sweetness she could have expired at the rapture. Fully aroused, he deepened the kiss, holding the back of her golden head to him so he could have more of her.

Little arrows of sexual yearning lanced deep into her body. They caused multiple involuntary contractions at the sensitive delta, as sharp and immediate as jabs of adrenalin. She didn't attempt to break away, though the level of passion was extremely high. She remained locked in his arms, a woman desperate for his kisses… He could do what he liked with her. She was a woman on fire. Absolutely aflame.

A howl of feline rage split them apart.

"I knew it. I knew it!" Marigole stood several feet away, dancing with pure jealousy. Her large dark eyes were almost starting out of her head. She was wearing an exquisite cream nightgown with a matching peignoir, the flawless skin she prized wax white with outrage.

Olivia was too shocked to feel embarrassment. Kissing wasn't a hanging offence. Even the passionate kissing that had generated such sizzling heat.

McAlpine predictably was swift to react. "Thank you, Marigole, for treating us to that howl. A wild dingo out there couldn't have done it better. Couldn't sleep?"

"You bastard!" she cried with ferocity, throwing back her peignoir so the outline of her body showed clearly through the near-transparent silk. "How could you? And with me in the house!"

Olivia came to her senses. These two people had been married for years. They knew each other intimately. Marigole had borne his child. He had admitted to an inescapable bond. Was it possible *she* was acting as a barrier to reunion? The woman still loved him. She even felt a pang of pity for her. It was a terrible thing to be unhappy whether one deserved it or not. And Marigole was dreadfully unhappy. So too was Georgy. She had been distraught at the divorce. Could she be in the way of causing the child further hurt?

Incredibly, even to her own ears, she sounded totally in command of herself. Long years of practise sometime came in handy. "I'll leave the two of you to talk."

"You're in love with him, aren't you?" Marigole cried, looking like a wild cat ready to use its claws.

"We shouldn't be talking when you're in this state, Mrs McAlpine," Olivia said, not without pity. "Sometimes a kiss *is* just a kiss, you know. I am *not* sleeping with Clint. That's your *ex*-husband?"

Marigole took a dancing pace towards her. "Think you're very clever, don't you?"

"Only about some things." Olivia stayed her hand from moving to her crystal. It was there for her to call on when needed. She could handle Marigole. At any rate, she thought she could. She had never figured in a love triangle.

"What say we call it a night?" McAlpine suggested briskly, apparently well used to Marigole, the drama queen. "Lucas no doubt is tucked up fast asleep in your bed, Marigole. I would remind you that both of you are guests in *my* house. And you're looking to me to take full custody of our daughter. I have to say, if you're looking to Lucas as your next husband, at least he'll be able to keep you in style. Now I suggest you stop going ballistic at the thought *I* might remarry."

Marigole's great dark eyes flashed lightning. "You have to be very, very careful with this man." White faced, she turned her attention back to the appalled Olivia. "He takes your heart, then he stomps on it. Why do you suppose I had to leave him?"

Was there something more to this than met the eye? Usually was. Sad to say.

"Not thinking clearly, Marigole." McAlpine's expression was frankly mocking. "If you haven't realised it yet, you will. We're *divorced*. It took you less than a week to take another lover."

"And what about *you*?" Hot colour stained her slanting cheekbones. "What about angel face here with the golden hair and the sapphire eyes and the so-posh voice. You've really been giving her the rush, haven't you? I bet it wasn't the course of action her father had in mind when he sent her."

Though rocked by Marigole's jealous rage, Olivia considered she had the right to intervene. "Either way, it's none of your business, Mrs McAlpine. *My* affairs are none of your business either. Let's keep it that way. I'll say goodnight."

"Good night, *Lady* Olivia," Marigole carolled after her. "Just don't make the mistake of thinking Clint can make you happy. He's a dangerous man. Believe me. You might have fallen for him hook, line and sinker—I'm not a fool—but you don't know him well at all."

Against the creamy skin of Olivia's breast, the flashing iridescent colours of her crystal had shaded into a pearly silver-grey.

It made her feel uneasy. Frightened too.

Marigole had made her point. She really didn't know McAlpine all that well.

CHAPTER EIGHT

For the first time since her arrival she slept very badly, turning this way and that, angry and miserable with Marigole's bad behaviour which in her view was right off the scale, quite manic. She was tormented too by her intense, unresolved desires interwoven with a natural worry about where things were heading.

Admit it. You're madly in love with him. Dangerous attraction.

But the question had to be asked. Was it the same for him as it was for her, given that men were even more sex driven than women? Only he would have had women falling at his feet from his teens. It couldn't be possible he was trying to manipulate her. Could it? She was, after all, a Balfour heiress. Even Justin had admitted she was quite a prize. A prize he hadn't acted on. But Justin was basically a society layabout, largely financed by his wealthy father.

McAlpine had turned his family fortune into the billions. Like her father he might be obsessed with making money. Again, like her father, a businessman first and last. Marriage in her world was too often a business arrangement with sex thrown in. Did McAlpine think like that? Marigole came from a wealthy family. He'd told her that himself.

Could history be repeating itself? It always did. No one actually *learned* from others' mistakes, or if they did they didn't put the learning into practise. Hadn't her mother, Alexandra, been the most beautiful and glamorous debutante of her time, a prize her father had swooped on without a moment's hesitation? Yet the marriage had been doomed to failure. Her father claimed Alexandra had betrayed him. Marigole claimed Clint had betrayed her. How exactly? Infidelity? Somehow she didn't think so.

Her mother must have been unhappily married, neglected by her workaholic husband. Was that the reason she had drifted into that fateful affair that had produced Zoe and left her dead? Even with his heart broken, her father had swiftly moved on. To other women. There were always other women in his life.

Would there always be other women in McAlpine's life? She couldn't help drawing parallels between two magnetic men who had power over women.

Was it any wonder the old insecurity beset her?

Breakfast went well. Everyone was in good spirits. It restored a measure of normality Afterwards Georgy, who had not breakfasted with the rest of them, bounded through her open bedroom door, her beautiful face, so alike yet so unlike her mother's, full of excitement. "Daddy said we're going out to Carlee Waters to spot you a croc. That's after lunch when the crocs take their siestas on the banks."

"I'll go on one condition." Olivia smiled, having already heard about the expedition. "The croc doesn't make *me* its lunch and you hold tight to my hand."

"Of course I will." Georgy went to her and gave her a spontaneous hug. "Please don't be worried. We'll be quite safe in the boat. Oh, Liv, it's going to be *wild*! They're so *hideous*, but so fascinating. Daddy would never let you come to any harm. Besides, the boat operator has the crocodile for his totem. That makes him the croc's brother."

"We don't have crocodiles in England."

"*No* wild animals?" Georgy questioned, thinking there had to be one or two.

"Unless you count our fearsome hedgehogs. I think someone reported seeing a death adder in a forest one time. Personally I think he was having us on."

"Where we're going there's tons of wildlife," Georgy said.

"You'll be amazed at all the birds. Thousands and thousands of them. All the wildfowl. You know we couldn't grow rice up here in the Territory for all the magpie geese. Even the air force couldn't warn them off. You'll see the water buffalo, great stupid things. They do a lot of damage. You won't see a camel, although there are plenty of them on Kalla Koori, but we might get to see a pair of brolgas—that's the blue cranes—dancing for us on the flats. You don't have to be scared of the crocs, Liv. Did you know more people die every year from bee stings than they do from crocodile attacks? Anyway, we're in the dry. It's September through January when they get *really* hungry. They're preparing to breed, you see."

"I'll remember that, Georgy," Olivia said, enjoying the child's excitement.

Georgy chatted on happily, clearly seeing Olivia as a friend.

"Have you seen your mother this morning?" Olivia asked in the first pause.

"Mummy never gets up early." Georgy's expression abruptly darkened. "She has to have her beauty sleep. Silly old Lucas is up though. He's dying to go on the trip."

Oh, dear! That could mean Marigole, whose image for Olivia was marginally less frightening than that of a crocodile, would be going along.

Wear your magic crystal.

No need to tell her that.

"You don't like Lucas?"

"Don't care for him at all," Georgy said with a frown. "He's smarmy and he's fat and *old*. Always trying to get me to like him. I never shall. All Mummy cares about is money. She got millions out of Daddy, the house in Sydney, the penthouse at the Gold Coast, but it's not enough. She wants everything in the world. Except *me*. Kids aren't part of her world, you see. She wants to stay young and beautiful for ever. She told me."

"But that's not possible for any of us, Georgy. Life is a journey.

We age and move on. Eventually we have to move aside for the next generation."

"*I* know that," Georgy cried with high emotion, showing Olivia another side of her, "but Mummy doesn't. When I'm not hating her I feel very sorry for her."

"You can't hate your mother, Georgy," Olivia said gently, having missed her mother all her life.

"I can!" the child shouted, then turned and ran out of the room.

They were out on the four-mile billabong, Carlee Waters, a great glittering sheet of water shaded on either bank by massive trees laced with the native honeysuckle, side by side with the ubiquitous stands of pandanus. Day after day, since her arrival, had dawned brilliantly fine, peacock-blue skies. This was, after all, the dry. And today was no exception. As Georgy had promised there were birds everywhere—flying, floating, wading, playing. Ducks, egrets, the infamous black and white magpie geese, the graceful blue cranes—though none danced for them—and legions of white ibis. There were great flotillas of blue lotus, the birds poking their long necks into the succulent bulbs. Lucas had his very expensive camera out, taking photograph after photograph, crying out after each, "Jolly good shot!" like a man on a golf course. On these occasions Georgy gave Olivia a conspiratorial smirk. Her good mood had been restored. Probably because her mother had elected to stay in bed and nurse her hangover.

Clint moved back to where Olivia, Georgy and Chloe were seated. His hand descended on Olivia's shoulder, tightening over the delicate bones. She turned up her beautiful face to him, blue eyes shining. He was deeply involved with her now. Extremely concerned Marigole had caused her further upset. Mercifully she looked quite serene. He pointed towards a tree alight with scarlet blossoms. "Snake python. It's just about to enter the water."

Olivia followed the direction of his pointing finger. The huge python had to be at least fourteen to fifteen feet long. It slithered across the white sand and swam into the emerald-green water.

"That's just a baby compared to the Queensland amethyst python," Georgy piped up gleefully. "Isn't it, Daddy?"

"That's right, sweetheart."

Olivia watched with approval as he gave his daughter a loving smile. No man who could smile at his daughter like that could be bad. Or all bad. "They attain around twenty feet and more. One has to steer clear of them. But our snake python is harmless to man."

"It's still an awesome sight!" Chloe's light soprano squeaked. In one way she was enthralled by the wild beauty of her surroundings, in another she was clearly terrified. She wouldn't have come, only she wanted to please Brendan. But she had expected a much bigger boat. *QE2* wouldn't have been too big. This was a little boat, a fishing boat really.

Olivia, in her big-sister mode, was keeping an eye on Chloe. Brendan certainly wasn't. It was Clint's company he most enjoyed. Peter Corbett had come along too. Barbara had elected to stay at home and swim in the beautiful infinity pool. Neil and Celine had had to leave shortly after lunch. She saw Peter was laughing uproariously at one of Brendan's jokes before beckoning to Clint to rejoin them.

Clint raised a lazy hand. "In a minute." His golden eyes glittered in the sun's rays. He let them roam over Olivia, his near-overwhelming desire for her just an inch beneath the surface. "Enjoying yourself?" His glance caressed her.

"This is a fantastic world." The answering expression in her blue eyes was melting, vulnerable.

"And look, Liv." Georgy made a grab for Olivia's hand. "There are our salties! They're having a snooze."

"Don't stand, or go to the side of the boat," Clint warned with a note of natural authority. "Just sit quietly and look."

They were about a quarter of a mile downstream, and there in the heat of the afternoon the giant saurians, the largest living reptiles and predators, armoured like tanks, were enjoying time out from snaffling everything in sight—mussels, crabs, fish, snakes, lizards, birds and their cohorts, flying foxes that lived in colonies nearby, all manner of unwary animals and the odd human crazy enough to invade their territory.

Chloe, scared out of her mind and filled with revulsion, muffled an involuntary four-letter word—she appeared to have a store of them—followed up quickly with, "They're revolting!"

Indeed they were, Olivia thought. Then again they exerted a powerful fascination. These were creatures that had remained relatively unchanged for more than two hundred million years. They had roamed the earth with the dinosaurs. Probably ate a few of them along the way.

"Sit still, Chloe," Clint repeated more sternly, thinking what a silly little thing Brendon had got mixed up with. "You're perfectly safe. Crocs aren't just good for expensive handbags, belts, shoes and luggage, the tails of the young crocs actually taste good. More like pork than fish."

"I've read that." Olivia took a hold of Chloe's rigid hand, willing her to relax. Georgy, following Olivia's example, took the other.

"We're going to have a feast of fresh barramundi tonight," Clint promised. It eased his heart to see his young daughter getting on so well with Olivia. Georgy had had little of her mother's company growing up. Olivia obviously had great rapport with the young. She was a deeper, finer, more compassionate woman altogether. She would make an excellent mother. He knew, when the time came, he would struggle to let her go. The end of her stay was still a long way away, but the time would fly by on gilded wings.

"See all the little ripples in the water, Liv?" Georgy was crying. "Barramundi."

"The finest-eating fish in the world!" McAlpine pronounced.

"But then you're a Territorian, Daddy!" Georgy looked up at her father with great love and pride. He was simply the best father in the world. And the most handsome.

Olivia, looking on, realised she had felt exactly the same

way about *her* father. McAlpine's manner, however, was much warmer, much more openly loving. That was his great gift.

An hour on and they were ready to return to the waiting helicopter.

"I've enjoyed this afternoon enormously," Olivia said, her expression mirroring the extent of her pleasure.

"Wish I could say the same," Chloe whispered from behind her hand. "It's way too wild for me. Those crocs! And the bats! Gosh, they stink, the ugly black things."

It was Clint who was navigating at this point, taking over from the skipper. He was keeping close to the near bank, while the skipper and Peter took care of the splendid barramundi catch.

Chloe stood and stretched, enormously relieved it was all over. Ironic, then; it was at this point all hell broke loose. A great flight of white cockatoos, the sentinels of the wild bush, screamed down the billabong like jets at an air show.

"Sit down, Chloe," Olivia cried out sharply as birds started to stream past the boat. "Sit down." What a time to be standing there, shaken and breathless. Olivia felt a sick, sliding sense of disaster in her stomach.

Yet all would have been well had Chloe shown some common sense, but instead of obeying Olivia, as any sensible person would, she totally lost her head. One might have thought they were war planes screaming down the billabong, instead of birds. Chloe let out a terrified scream as several of the birds tuned into her scream, broke formation and shot through one side of the boat to the other. Chloe continued screaming, holding her hands over her head, as though she was in a Hitchcock movie. Not satisfied, she pitched forward, hands still clasped over her head, stumbled into some loose tackle and sent the feather-light Georgy, who had been staring at her speechless, to reel backwards and, from there, pitch over the side.

"God!"

Olivia scarcely heard Chloe's horrified cry. She was taut with nerves and an in-flow of adrenalin. Without a moment's hesi-

tation she dived into the murky waters near the pier, making a
grab for Georgy and urging her towards the dinghy that had been
swiftly let down and was trailing in the water.

"Fast as you can!"

Georgy needed no urging. A good school-girl swimmer she
took off at a pace she had never achieved in her young life, with
Olivia, the much stronger swimmer, stroking hard alongside her
as her escort, ready and willing to give assistance.

It was Brendan, a big man, who hauled Georgy single-hand-
edly aboard. Olivia went for the dinghy, raising herself high on
her arms and clambering in. Above her Clint stood, rifle in hand,
his hands perfectly steady even under tremendous pressure, looking down the sights. He wasn't firing. He was *waiting*. A heroic
figure.

One bullet to the brain. He couldn't miss.

It seemed to Olivia like an eternity. She dared not turn her
head. She just knew a crocodile was propelling itself at great
speed towards the vulnerable dinghy with her lying in the bottom
of the small craft. Pure instinct told her to trust him. She knew
he was a crack shot. She *had* to trust him to pick the precise
moment. No time to pull her out of the dinghy. Her fingers found
her magic talisman, closed over the stone. She didn't feel in the
least stupid muttering a prayer for help. This stone had infernal
powers.

"Clint, Clint! It's goin' away!" The skipper, Milo, was yell-
ing at the top of his voice. "Don't shoot, man. Clint, please don't
shoot. Don't kill 'im. Ain't his fault. There's no danger ahead.
We'll get your brave missy into the boat now. Never seen nuthin'
like it. Look at that blue light on the water. Like a spear. Frighten
old man croc away."

It was impossible to get into the house without being met in
the entrance hall. Kath was the first to greet them, eyeing the
dishevelled party in shocked disbelief and concern. Marigole and
Barbara made their appearance within moments, Marigole with
her trademark shriek. McAlpine had stripped off his bush shirt

to envelop his daughter, exposing a magnificent bronzed torso of lean, hard muscle. Even his flat stomach was clad with muscle.

Milo had found a sarong-type garment belonging to his girl friend for Olivia to wrap herself in. She looked, had she known it, a tantalising sight.

Marigole, as was to be expected, worked herself within seconds into quite a state. Shockingly she didn't go to her daughter to hug her close. She stood aloof, starting to loudly assign blame. First and foremost to Clint, then Olivia, as though together they were responsible for the incident.

"Shut up, Marigole!" McAlpine turned on her in no uncertain terms. "You don't think our daughter might need some comfort from her mother?" His whole demeanour was so daunting even the foolhardy Marigole backed off hurriedly.

The most extraordinary thing was Georgy appeared to be in high spirits as though their "adventure" had geared her up several notches.

"I can't wait to tell my classmates!" she cheered. "It'll make a terrific story. Liv was just so *cool*! I reckon she should be given a medal."

But then Georgy was Territory born and raised and she hadn't seen the crocodile surging towards the dinghy. Her head was buried against her father's broad chest. Olivia hadn't sighted the fearsome predator zooming towards her either, but no way did she find the incident *cool*. She was very much on edge. So too was McAlpine. Such a grim expression was on his striking face. His mouth was set tight; a muscle along his jaw jumped, those wild-cat eyes blazing away with menace.

Kath moved with alacrity, whisking Georgy away for a shampoo and shower. "Don't worry about me, everyone," Georgy called. "I'm definitely OK!"

Thank the gods for that! With special mention of the Ancient One who gave the crystal life! A blue spear, the skipper had said. That made her wonder. And Milo wasn't the only one to see it. McAlpine had seen it too. Maybe only certain people could take mystic readings?

Brendan was gradually calming poor Chloe, whose tear-laden admissions of guilt Marigole had ignored entirely. Brendan was clearly regretting the fact he had allowed his girlfriend to go along for the trip. He led her away, one arm around her narrow, shaking shoulders. Brendan had arrived in his private plane with their friends Peter and Barbara in tow. Now he agreed to fly Marigole and Lucas back with them to Darwin. They could make their own way from there. Lucas had mentioned taking Marigole for a stay at Queensland's glorious Port Douglas. Maybe he wasn't so keen now?

Safely in her room, Olivia all but collapsed against the closed door. She had been fine up until now. Only to be expected that a reaction would set in. Like Georgy she would take a shower and shampoo the dank salt water out of her now-riotously curling hair.

A knock on the door brought her away from it. She turned, then tentatively opened it, prepared to see Marigole and have her start up her wild accusations again. Only McAlpine stood framed in the doorway, as splendid a wild man as any woman was likely to lay eyes on. He hadn't even bothered to find a shirt. Obviously there were far more important things on his mind.

"I just had to check you're OK?" he said tersely. His eyes were moving all over her—her face, her bare shoulders, her tall, slender body bound by the hot-pink sarong.

Sensation poured into her intoxicated heart. What chemistry this man had! "A little shaky, nothing more. You look angry?" In fact, he looked as fierce as any tribal warrior.

"I am angry," he gritted with a clash of his fine white teeth. "Bren never learns. He lost the one woman he loved, now he goes from one lightweight chick to the other. He should have known Chloe had the potential to freak out."

"Well, she's suffering now," Olivia said. "Poor Chloe. I have to feel sorry for her. It was a tough lesson."

"Please!" He cracked one fist into the palm of his hand. "I don't want to hear about, Chloe. She'll be over it soon enough. None of us puts any blame on her. Georgy is handling this.

Thank God kids are so resilient. They can pick up after escaping from the most dangerous situations. It's you I'm worried about. Marigole is right. I have to take full responsibility for the whole sorry incident."

"It's over, Clint." Always the peace maker, she sought to soothe him, recognising his extreme upset. Looking after people had been one of his great strengths. "All's well that ends well, don't they say?"

He turned on his heel. "I'll go. You don't need me here."

She moved after him, impelled to do so. She placed a gentle hand on his broad, naked shoulder and left it there. "I might look a bit shaken now, Clint, but I promise you this hasn't put me off. I *will* go out on Carlee Waters again." And she meant it. Not quite as easy as getting back on a horse after a bad spill, but she knew she could do it.

He wheeled, high tension flashing off him in currents. "Not with me, you won't!" he rasped. "Do you even *know* how I feel?"

"Tell me." She stared up into his dazzling eyes, as passionate in her way as he was in his.

"Tell? Why don't I *show* you?"

He spun her so she had her back to the door, hauling her up against him. His expression was a black scowl, as though he had lost his habitual control and been taken over by his own personal demon. His head, a tousled mass of deep waves, bent low over hers. "I want to make love to you," he said harshly, in no way loverlike. "I want to make never-ending love to you. I want to make love to you on a scale you can't even imagine."

Fierce as he looked, so charged with testosterone, she wasn't in the least afraid. She might have been as vulnerable to him as the antelope to the lion, but she had never felt so alive or so physically aware—sensations so new to her she found them as liberating as they were overwhelming. She wanted this from the deepest, most primitive part of her being—the part of her that operated on the most basic sexual impulses. God, hadn't she waited long enough?

His strong arms were lashed around her, though she realised he was only using a small part of his strength. Even so, she twisted her body slightly to ease his hold, an involuntary little cry escaping her throat. Instantly he lessened the pressure. But he wouldn't let go. She had no wish to break away. Rather, there was no conflict. She was revelling in the sensation of physical helplessness, woman against the dominant male.

Mouths and bodies were locked together in a passionate embrace, tongues probing, flicking, exploring, in incredible sensual pleasure. It was as violent a sexual confrontation as she had ever imagined. Elemental forces were at work. The knot on her sarong had worked itself loose. The cotton garment slid to her hips, where it rested precariously. There was the inevitability it would slip to the floor but she couldn't seem to care. She hadn't removed her sodden clothing totally. Wet or not she had kept on her flimsy briefs. They had dried out in less than ten minutes in the tropical heat.

Still holding her mouth with his, he let his hands move down compulsively over the satin-smooth globes of her naked breasts, caressing the contours, taking their weight in his hands, allowing her erect nipples to brush against his chest hair.

The pleasure was frightening and immense. "Oh, God!" she whispered frantically into his mouth, so sexually aroused she wouldn't have made a move to stop him if he decided to take her there and then on the carpet. Nothing she had known was anything like this. This was the one thing that mattered and, so far, that she had missed out on. No wonder her development as a woman had been stunted.

Except he stopped dead. He jerked his head back, mentally if not physically distancing himself from her. She was amazed at the change in him, deeply at a loss. A great shudder ran through his powerful body. "I'm sorry, Olivia," he groaned. "Forgive me. I'm losing it. I'm ashamed. So ashamed. I shouldn't be touching you. Marigole is right. This isn't what your father intended."

His hands reached blindly for the sarong. He brought the

hot-pink fabric up over her breasts, unchallenged by the way to tie it.

"I just had to see how you were. I was frantic. Things have got out of hand. The last thing I want is to destroy our friendship. I'll never forget how you dived in after Georgy with no thought for your own safety. That truly proves your worth, Olivia, if it even needed proving. You're a fine woman, a fine human being." He lifted her right hand and pressed a kiss into her palm. "Forgive me?" he begged tautly, visibly pale beneath his dark tan.

She nodded, totally bereft of words.

After he had gone she threw herself down on the bed. Giving enormous pleasure didn't require forgiveness surely? How did one go about forgiving the best thing that had ever happened to her? Such had been his influence on her that she had already undergone significant changes. She was warmer, more loving, more open. Less self-protective, less concerned with preserving an "image" at all costs. Her image was phoney anyway. She understood now that, to a large extent, she had been controlled. Her rewards had been her father's ongoing approval. There had been no higher authority in her life.

Until now.

You love him, Olivia. You really love him.

Even if nothing could come from it—they lived in very different worlds—it was Clint McAlpine who had brought the real Olivia into being.

CHAPTER NINE

CLINT had told them he would be away for about a fortnight. The fortnight spun out into a month of tough business negotiations. Or was he taking his time about coming back to her? Olivia spent time agonising over that. Could he be determined on a clear break, perhaps finding his feelings too complex? He was right about one thing. Things between them had escalated in furious leaps and bounds. Relationships either went forward or they broke down and fell apart. That wasn't happening here. Not yet. The great bonus for her was he had soothed her troubled heart. He respected her. His respect was important to her. But he had warned her he wasn't going to rush into a second marriage.

"Only an idiot would make the same mistake twice!"

Who could blame him? From all accounts, sweet as honey at the beginning, Marigole had along the way developed into a very difficult, self-centred and totally unlikeable woman. Her biggest failing was she had cut off her only child, in all probability the major factor in the breakdown of the marriage.

As the days and nights passed, she moved from inner questions to a variety of possible answers, obsessing really, her whole being taken over by her deep feelings for him. Kath had refused point-blank to take the holiday Clint had promised her and her husband.

"It's like a holiday having you around, Livvy!"

So Kath had stayed on, claiming she had as good as adopted Olivia. Certainly they were very easy on each other's company. Olivia had made it her business to spend time with everyone on the station—the most powerful of all, Eerina aka Bessie, who showed herself from time to time. Bessie's work as an artist was very important to her. It often took her on desert walkabouts.

Ever-conscientious Olivia had turned her attentions to Georgy. Maybe as daughters of powerful fathers with huge claims on their time and interest, their identification had come easily. Also there was the missing-mother factor. Olivia recognised her life would have been very different had her mother lived. Georgy *had* her mother, though her mother behaved as if her only child was somehow unrelated to her. Marigole, physically beautiful but spiritually lacking, had wanted a son, as a symbol of achievement. No wonder Georgy had moved quite a way down the path of maladjustment. In the time she was on the station Olivia was determined on helping Georgy work out strategies to cope.

First came the riding lessons. Georgy was terrified of horses. Initially Olivia had found that impossible to believe until Kath told her on the quiet about the sort of "lessons" Marigole had given her. That is to say, Marigole had been so sharp and impatient, so scathing of her daughter's seeming lack of ability, the two of them reached the stage where Marigole stated flatly her daughter would *never* make a rider. It was adult intolerance of a child at the highest and worst level.

The first requirement of a good teacher is undoubtedly patience. And lots of it. Olivia had patience in spades. That one quality made all the difference in the world. With no Marigole to berate her and strip her of all confidence, Georgy was able to relax and proceed comfortably each day with her lessons. Olivia, who found horses the most beautiful of all animals, had little difficulty communicating that love to Georgy, who had progressed to reaching out, touching, petting, feeding from the hand and generally conveying her gentleness to the small, sweet-tempered mare Olivia had picked out for her.

"You're a miracle worker, that's what you are!" Kath declared happily over a companionable cup of tea. "You need kids of your own, love. You'll make a wonderful mother. You're so kind and patient and so understanding of children. I've never known Georgy to be so at peace."

It was obvious to them all. Olivia, a woman with a strong academic bent, had been supervising Georgy's study program which had been sent on to her by her school. Georgy was a highly intelligent child. She would be ready to start the new term in August. And the core area of conflict had been removed with Marigole's departure.

"Clint will shape his daughter's life," said Kath. "The thing is, he has to work so hard. He has enormous responsibilities. He needs a wife." Kath peered hard into Olivia's blue eyes.

"Don't look at me, Kath," Olivia responded with a deep telling blush.

"I *am* looking at you, love. The two of you would be perfect, even if you can't see it yet. You wouldn't be stuck in the wilds, if that part is important to you."

"But it isn't, Kath," Olivia protested. "I love it here."

Kath's eyes were thoughtful. "Clint leads a very busy social life from time to time and he travels a great deal. He needs a woman. A woman like *you* who can take her place anywhere. Buckingham Palace, I reckon."

Olivia had to laugh.

"You know what I mean, love," said Kath, patting her hand. "Now Bessie said an odd thing the other day."

Olivia felt the onset of tingles. "What was it?"

"Can't say, love. Bessie just run it by me. I wouldn't want to be the one to break one of Bessie's confidences. Gawd knows what would happen to me. Bessie's a sorceress."

"Tell me about it," Olivia said, ready to accept it was Eerina's magic crystal that had caused the blue spear to hurtle into Carlee Waters.

As it was, Clint surprised them. He hadn't let anyone know he was returning, so when Olivia and Georgy came in from their riding lesson, faces glowing with achievement, there he was strolling down the portico towards them.

"Daddy!" Georgy's voice rang out with happiness. She went into his outstretched arms, receiving a warm kiss and a hug. "Why didn't you tell us you were coming back?"

"The answer's simple, sweetheart. I wanted to surprise you." McAlpine lifted his gleaming head to acknowledge Olivia. "How are you, Olivia?"

Not showing it on the outside, inside she was aglow. "I'm fine, thank you, Clint. And you?"

"Missing my womenfolk."

"You mean Liv and me?" Georgy looked up at him with startled eyes.

"Don't forget Kath."

"Oh, we missed *you*!" Georgy cried, hugging him again.

Over his daughter's head, McAlpine's golden gaze on Olivia was very intent.

He appeared to be checking off her features one by one. Relearning them?

Did he know his return had rekindled the blaze in her? He looked marvellous, radiating his special brand of male vitality.

"Liv has been teaching me to ride," Georgy confided. "She's a great teacher. Not a bit like Mum calling me stupid all the time."

"You've been an excellent pupil." Olivia smiled, transferring her blue gaze to Clint. "When you've got time, Clint, Georgy would love to show you what she can do."

"What's this, time?" he jeered. "Of course I've got time. I can't wait to see you up on a horse, my darling." He drew Georgy under his shoulder. "What say we have lunch and afterwards we can go back down to the stables? Suit you, *Liv*?" An amused smile played around his sexy mouth.

"I wouldn't miss it for the world."

Don't go back into your shell, girl. This is your time for transformation. Your time to rethink your life. Remake it. Look to the future.

One thing she was sure of. Her future wasn't going to be along the same lines as her past.

* * *

For a few weeks McAlpine changed his routine so he could spend more time with them, though his workload was considerable. Olivia realised he was catching up long after the household had retired. The various McAlpine operations had offices everywhere, but McAlpine naturally made it his business to oversee everything, just as Olivia's father did. It was very much hands-on.

"Look, I'm pretty smart actually," Olivia said one evening over dinner.

"Sure is!" Georgy piped up. "She knows more than my teachers."

"You're biased, Georgy." Olivia smiled. "I've been helping Georgy with her schoolwork," she told McAlpine.

"I know."

She couldn't quite fathom the expression on his dynamic face. "I speak fluent French and Italian and I can get by with my German."

"Good Lord, is there no end to your talents!" McAlpine exclaimed, refilling her wineglass.

"I told you she was clever." Georgy nodded owlishly. "Can I have a drop of that, Daddy?"

"No, my darling, you can't," McAlpine told her firmly. "You've got a good few more years to go yet and then only in moderation."

"Tell that to Mummy." Georgy sighed. "Even silly old Lucas has told her to stop."

"Good for Lucas," said McAlpine crisply.

"I'd like to help if I could." Olivia took up the thread. "I do have a good business head. All of us do, as a matter of fact."

"Liv has a *huge* family," Georgy told her father, clearly envious. "Her father, Oscar, sent them all over the world to find themselves. Isn't that strange? I mean you're *you* wherever you are."

McAlpine's eyes were on Olivia's porcelain-skinned face. "Sometimes it's easier to find one's identity in a new environment. I hope Olivia will agree with that?"

"I do." She met the searching eyes. "I love the freedom here. And I've loved being of help to you." She reached out to touch Georgy's hand.

"So why don't you stay?" Georgy asked in the sweetest, winning way. "You don't have to rush off home."

"Olivia has to return to England for her father's birthday," McAlpine reminded her. "It's going to be a big reunion party."

"I don't think I'm going to like it when you're gone, Liv." Georgy stood, abruptly pushing back her chair.

"I've promised you, you can always come and visit me, Georgy." Olivia looked up with concern at the suddenly downcast child.

"I'm frightened I'll never see or hear of you again if you go away."

"You have my promise that won't happen." Solemnly Olivia crossed her heart.

"I know you mean it, Liv."

"I do."

"OK." Georgy brightened. "That's all right, then. May I be excused?"

"Of course you may, sweetheart," McAlpine said.

"I'm going to finish my book—never get tired of rereading it, *Jane Eyre*—then I'm planning a deep sleep. I'm getting more exercise with my riding than I have in my whole life."

"I'll come and tuck you in," McAlpine called after her.

"Bring Liv with you." Georgy made off with a little wave.

Olivia started learning about McAlpine Enterprises that very night. Clint was working his way through endless piles of paperwork he didn't entrust to anyone else. Just like her father. In many ways they were a pair. It struck her that her father would have given anything to have a son like McAlpine. Tradition, the father-son bond, all that.

"You can trust me." She was peering over his shoulder as he sat at his desk. "Even if you only let me take charge of your personal life, a kind of confidential secretary. I could wade through all those invitations you receive, check with you, accept some, decline others, look after household accounts. Less for the office to do. I could remember family birthdays, send off cards, presents, that sort of thing. You get piles of letters, memos, documents, et cetera. Father does too. Why not let me wade through them?"

He turned his head to stare up at her. Her beautiful hair was loose, falling seductively from a centre part to curve onto her cheeks, then flow over her shoulders. He wanted to grab her and pull her down to him, only she coloured and straightened. "Why, are you bored?" He watched her round his massive partner's desk to take a leather armchair opposite.

"Not at all!" she assured him when she could trust herself to speak. "But I *was* sent to help out in some way."

"You've worked wonders with Georgy," he told her quietly.

"It's been a real pleasure." The thought of having to leave here was indeed occupying much of her mind. The future was so indistinct. "Georgy's a lovely girl. Highly intelligent. I meant what I said—I'll remain her friend for as long as she wants. You know she has to go back to school. We've kept up with the curriculum, even gone ahead, but she has to return. The longer she stays at home, the harder it will be to go back. I think she's ready."

"I was getting around to discussing it with her, Olivia. She's missing her friend, Kristy."

Olivia smiled. "The one who sends all the emails?"

Clint's hands locked behind his gleaming head. "They started boarding school together. Kristy used to holiday with us fairly frequently, only Marigole found her irritating. God knows why. Kristy is a great kid. By the way, we'll have visitors for next weekend, a Texan rancher with his wife—David and Alexa Arnold. He's a mining magnate, nice guy. He'll be bringing a business associate from Hong Kong with his lady friend of the moment. It should be fun."

"Leave it to me," said Olivia. "So do I get to help you out or not?"

He pinned her with his brilliant gaze. "You're helping me just by being here, Olivia. But OK, I have a lot of faith in you."

"I'm not a Balfour for nothing." Did he know how much his trust gratified her?

His laugh was brief. "Are you going to keep the Balfour when you marry, or lose it entirely?"

Olivia Balfour-McAlpine. Now that had a lovely ring to it. *Dream on.*

"I'll leave a pile of stuff for you to wade through," he said, looking back at a stack of files. "See what you make of it. I'll be flying to Darwin midmorning for an extended business meeting. Looking for investors for a new building project."

"I'm sure you'll rope them in."

"Thank you for the vote of confidence. We have pearling interests too, as you now know. I may stay overnight depending on how things go, but I'll be back in a couple of days."

Just a glimmer of his dazzling smile, but it made her heart contract. "Take care." She meant it from the bottom of her heart. All this flying was worrying her. Here it was a way of life.

"A smile would be better."

"Take care, McAlpine," she repeated, eyes bluer than blue, a smile, unconsciously poignant, curving her lips.

You're too far gone to ever, ever forget him.

"And *you* take care." He rose as she did, coming towards her. "How I stop myself from coming for you in the night, I don't know," he muttered, something in his tone indicating enforced acceptance.

"But where would it get us, Clint?"

Only seething emotions, obliterating sensation.

"It would get us to confront what we feel for each other," he answered in a clipped voice. "I can't bear the thought of your leaving, yet I can see that you hear home calling. I realise you need to think long and hard about taking great risks."

"And the risk is *you*?"

"You already know the answer to that." His hands lifted to caress the slopes of her shoulders. "We didn't choose each other.

You had your life. I had mine. It was destiny that brought us together. The big question is, when you get home will you forget about even being here?"

"Never!" She spoke so softly it was almost under her breath.

"So it's in my best interests to give you plenty to remind you."

She lifted her face, knowing even the act of leaving him to fly home would be unbearable. But he was testing her. And testing her hard. He had had a bad experience. There could be no more of that.

He trapped her body against his, crushing her breasts to his chest. Then he was kissing her with great abandon, just as she was returning his passionate kisses with a hunger to equal his. It was a huge effort to break apart. A huger effort not to begin to throw off their clothes so they could glory in naked skin against skin.

He took his hands from her. Both of them were trembling. She whispered his name but it seemed to be a point of honour with him not to seduce her while she was beneath his roof. She was going home. Back to her old life. Neither of them could ignore that.

Least of all McAlpine. It was a huge temptation not to rush her. Take her to bed. He knew she would come willingly. His body was in a torment of sexual frustration but he saw clearly he had to protect her until she was very sure of her own mind. England was a long way off. She had to be given the opportunity to return to her glittering world. And only then would she be in a position to decide.

Her father had never allowed her more than a glimpse into his complex business dealings. He had been notoriously secretive. She knew the Balfour Foundation had an endless list of beneficiaries. Her father had to be one of the biggest philanthropists in the country. She met with a similar set-up with McAlpine Enterprises. The pastoral arm was only one of a wide portfolio of interests. When she found something a little difficult—these weren't ordinary business affairs; this was big business—he found time to explain things to her. He not only directed her, he gave her reasons for what he was doing. He was even asking her opinion on a range of issues. One, a high-risk investment she thought mightn't have been necessary given McAlpine Enterprises' high rate of growth.

"Chip off the old block, Olivia!" He smiled, thinking she could become an enormous asset.

"Sons are expected to be chips off the old blocks. Not daughters."

"Oscar should have started you off at a junior executive level. It wouldn't have taken you long to rise to the top."

"You're joking!"

He looked back at her seriously. "Not at all. I've got top people who aren't as sharp as you are. Your mind leaps so briskly ahead, you've been able to cover a lot of ground in a very short time. Oscar's loss."

When the time came, the two of them delivered Georgy to her prestigious girl's college where she was greeted royally. Several of her girlfriends were on hand to welcome her back for the new term.

"I must say Georgina is looking particularly well," the headmistress gushed, beaming on Georgina's stunning father, a flush of pleasure in her cheeks. "She is one of our most promising students."

"You won't go home without coming to see me?" Georgy had made Olivia promise.

"Count on it," Olivia said, returning the child's emotional hug. "And you'll be coming to see me in England."

"Oh, I will! But I'm hoping you'll want to come back to us, after you see your dad and your sisters. Bessie said you would."

"When was this?" Olivia was startled.

"The day she called in with that great billabong painting she did for you."

"She never said anything to me."

"Gosh, no. You're not supposed to know. Just slipped out. That's why I'm so happy—you'll be coming back."

Physical pain started up in her chest. And an intense hope. However badly one wanted something it didn't always happen. She was in love with McAlpine. She knew he was very strongly attracted to her. What would her father make of it? The relationship mightn't suit him at all.

It's your life, girl.

That evening she and Clint were to attend an art showing at one of the city's leading galleries—a relatively new young artist who had been receiving serious attention from the critics. Supper at an art patron's river-side mansion was to follow, the guest list drawn up with particular care.

Olivia spent a couple of hours of the afternoon having her hair done before choosing a cocktail dress at a boutique that had been recommended to her. She wanted to look her very best, as a woman wants to look her most beautiful for the man she loves.

CHAPTER TEN

OLIVIA loved art. She had been attending art showings all her life. Some of the world's finest galleries were open to the English public and overseas tourists for free. From time to time one of her jobs had been to open certain showings.

The new young artist's work was not particularly to her liking for all the critical acclaim. The canvases were huge. Maybe that was it. The bigger, the better? The style abstract. One could get away with nearly anything if one stuck to the abstract. These days "traditional art," where one actually had to be able to draw and apply paint, was almost the kiss of death with some galleries and critics. She didn't like the way the paint had been trowelled on either. Or the dreary monochrome colours.

"Our artist ought to hose it all off and start again," Clint seconded her opinion. "Oh, for God's sake, don't look now."

"What is it?" For an appalled moment she thought the artist might have been hovering near and overhead Clint's comment.

"Marigole and Lucas," Clint groaned. "I thought they were still at Port Douglas."

"Not bothering you, is it?" She stared up into his handsome face. He didn't look so much perturbed as disgusted.

"Not if it doesn't bother you. I would guess they've been invited to the supper. Do you really want to go?"

"Not if *you* don't."

"How we are in accord." He smiled down at her. In his view she was far and away the most beautiful and stylish woman in a room full of glamorous, expensively dressed women. But none had her finely wrought classical features or her taut, slender body. And those long legs! Her hairstyle was new to him, side parted, with layers that kicked up in deep waves. It was enormously sexy. Her dress was short, above the knee, one-shouldered. He loved the Grecian look on her, the colour a heavenly shade of blue to match her eyes. She wore exquisite drop earrings, oval sapphires set in diamonds. He had never seen them before. Had she recently bought them? Lord knows she was an heiress.

"Let's beat it into the next room," he murmured, taking her arm. "With any luck at all we may not run into them as there's such a crush."

No such luck!

Marigole, the consummate actress, with so many very curious eyes on her, greeted her ex-husband with a kiss on both cheeks, resting one small delicate hand on his black-jacketed shoulder.

"Lovely to see you!" She included Olivia in her bright smile. "Georgina's back in school." It wasn't a question. She *knew*. "I'm dying to see her."

"A pity, Marigole," Clint said, his expression cool but hardening. "Because she doesn't want to say one word to you. I'd advise you to stay away and wait until she wants to see you."

"If you say so, darling. I only want her to be happy."

"She *is* happy," Clint said.

Marigole turned her ice-black eyes on Olivia. "Love the hair. And the dress. Go to Sonya's, did you? She always stocks the best. Haven't got long to go now." She gave a throaty laugh. "When is your father's birthday again?"

Olivia retained her social smile. It came easily after years of the most intensive practise. "I'm sure, Marigole, you already know."

"So touchy!" Marigole pouted. "Anyway, I wish you well. I'm sorry we didn't get off to a good start. If you were staying in the country we could start again. You've been very good for Georgina. I do appreciate it. She's been sending me progress reports. Ah, there's dear Lucas. I expect we'll be seeing you at the supper?" She lifted her eyes to her splendid ex-husband.

"Afraid not, Marigole," he said smoothly. "We're moving on to another function. In fact, we're leaving right now."

Progress reports? Olivia pondered. Was it possible Georgy had been sending her mother progress reports? Lord knows she sent enough emails. Clint might have been eyeing Marigole with huge disbelief, but she felt a deep pang akin to desolation. A mother is a mother after all. Marigole mightn't have been of much comfort to her young daughter with her abrasive ways and quick temper, but surely the mother-daughter bond could never be broken? She had friends who couldn't stand their mothers, but all of them would claim to love them. Maybe *liking* one's mother wasn't strictly necessary? It was a terribly sobering thought. Georgy might, at the back of her mind, be hoping for a reconciliation between her parents. Why else send her mother progress reports?

Nothing is simple or straightforward in this life, Olivia.

If the voice turned to issuing emails, she would delete them.

It took quite a while before they were able to leave the gallery. Clint knew so many people who stopped him for a few words and to gain an introduction to his companion. Before they left he made his apologies to the society hostess who was genuinely upset he and Olivia—by now they all knew who she was, or rather who her father was—couldn't join them.

It wasn't yet eight o'clock. "Let's go some place and have dinner," Clint suggested. "I know just the spot. Nicely out of the way."

"Don't want to be seen with me?" Olivia asked, unaware her flawless skin was blooming in the street lights, her sumptuous mane like a halo.

"How could you even say such a thing! I'm terrified Marigole is going to chuck supper and follow our cab."

Mercifully that didn't happen.

It was one of those intimate little places that served wonderful food. Clint ordered a bottle of vintage Bollinger the moment they sat down. "If Marigole attempts to upset Georgy I'll break her neck."

"You think she will?"

Remember, love and hate go together.

"Oh, you don't know, Marigole," he said, a tautness to his expression.

"Do you think Georgy really has been emailing her mother? The progress reports she mentioned. Marigole is her mother after all."

"After all, what?" he said disgustedly. "After all the rotten years? Don't let's talk about Marigole. I'm sick to death of the woman. Sorry if that sounds bad, but that's the way it is."

"I'm sorry," she said. "I've seen so much heartache in my life. My father has suffered and he has inflicted suffering in turn. But I love him. Nothing can change that."

"Men aren't in the race when it comes to devious behaviour," he said tersely.

"Not true. I've known plenty of devious liars. All male."

"I guess." He turned his golden eyes on her and smiled. "If it's worrying you, I'm certain Georgy hasn't been sending her mother any progress reports."

"I wish I could believe that." A shadow fell across her face.

"Easy enough to check."

"I wouldn't spy on Georgy," she said, horrified. "All of us love our parents no matter what they do."

He made a little scoffing sound beneath his breath. "Georgy has a tougher streak than you. She's lived in a different world. Kids these days question their parents' morality. They're bright, they're outspoken, they're not afraid to express their views. Georgy doesn't hate her mother. No one wants that, least of all me, because hate is corrosive. But Georgy knows her mother doesn't love her. Whatever your father's ideas and the way of life he has in a sense imposed on you, he loves you. Huge difference there."

It was a bit of a stretch—a couple of city blocks—but they decided to walk back to their hotel. It was a beautiful balmy night, the city humming with activity, tourists and locals strolling about. Lining the way were leafy trees decorated with tiny shimmering white lights. The huge picture windows of the shops, the upscale boutiques, the high-rises and the cars all reflected a kaleidoscope of colour and glitter. With so many milling around on the streets—happy, prosperous, well-dressed people—he kept her close to his side to avoid her being inadvertently knocked.

For all the cooling river breezes, she could feel the heat of desire spread over her skin like the heat off a fire. It seemed extraordinary to her she had to wait until she was twenty-eight before experiencing a true sexual awakening. And he hadn't even taken her to his bed! Yet there was a bond between them that had grown stronger. Was it possible that bond would snap when she had to return to the other side of the world?

Absence makes the heart grow fonder—or out of sight, out of mind? Take your pick!

Such was her involvement with Clint McAlpine at *all* levels; her former life had all but faded from her mind. It seemed, all at once, incredible what had passed between them.

Lively conversation had flowed while they were out on the street, but inside their hotel both of them abruptly went quiet. Glancing at him in the elevator his striking face wore an oddly steely expression, as though he was forcing himself to do something he didn't really want to do.

What exactly?

A man at war with himself? She felt a sense of foreboding. Did he have something to tell her? Something that might possibly break her heart? There *was* a woman. Not Marigole? A woman who might fit more easily into his lifestyle. Not a woman who bore the badge of the British aristocratic elite.

He saw her to her door, his handsome face a dark golden mask. Hiding God knows what? she pondered. "Sleep well, Olivia." He dipped his head to lightly brush her cheek. "I'll pick you up for breakfast, say eight o'clock? I thought we'd take a car tour around the city and its sights before we head back to Kalla Koori."

What is he hiding from you? What is it he won't say?

"Good night, Clint." She gave him a real smile. "Thank you for a lovely evening." There was something odd about his manner she couldn't quite put a finger on. If only she were a more sexually confident woman she might have thought he didn't want the night to end there. Only she had to make the first move.

You're way out of your depth.

She watched him walk away down the corridor—tall, wide shoulders, slim hipped, his body the perfect male model. Though he would have hated to be told that. She knew his room number. She had made the bookings.

Why do you always abide by the conventions? Why do you always play it safe? You were up for all those passionate kisses. What sense is there in jamming on the brakes? You're twenty-eight, for God's sake! Such reticence is laughable.

She simply couldn't believe a man could kiss one woman with so much ardour but have another woman in mind for a wife.

You know what Bella always says. Men are brutes!

McAlpine wasn't a brute.

The true depth of your relationship is obviously bothering him.

He's trying to minimise the dangers? For all the intensity of their attraction she might turn out to be someone transient in his life? Her father had sent her to him, believing she would be in safe hands.

Maybe he's being extra-scrupulous? Maybe he's holding himself under tremendous constraint? Damn it, girl, he could be waiting for some sign from you.

She couldn't contain her restlessness. She threw off her beautiful blue dress, catching sight of herself in the long mirror. She touched her breast, staring back at herself. Her *new* self. It might have been a trick of the light but she looked beautiful. Rather like Bella.

What if you tippy-toed down the corridor and knocked on his door? Make up some excuse? Anything. Say you'll be taking an early morning jog. Just wanted to let him know.

Before what little confidence she had collapsed, she pulled

a long caftan she had brought with her over her head. She had thought at the time the silk was just begging to be touched. She was quivering with nerves, preparing to encounter resistance, possible humiliation.

By the time she was out in the hallway—mercifully no one was around—she was marvelling at her own daring. Anyone would think she was underage, instead of overage. She had stayed for weekends in many country houses, back home, but she had never been one for bed hopping. She had always been expected to do the right thing. It had enslaved her. And where exactly had it got her? Men soon lost interest in women who only did the right thing.

Time to find out!

By the time she reached his door she was nearly fainting with a great surfeit of emotion.

Pull yourself together. You can deal with it.

Only the hand she put out to tap on his door went limp. He could well be asleep.

Oh, don't be so stupid.

Even the voice in her head was egging her on. Both of them sick of her procrastination. Yet she could hardly breathe. To her horror she stopped just short of pounding on his door such was the excess of adrenalin.

You're on your own now, girl. Don't make a mess of it.

He opened it, looked down at her, golden eyes blazing, then without a word slid a strong arm around the small of her back and pulled her with great urgency into his room.

"Clint, I…"

She felt the burn of his glance. "Hush." He kissed her then, fierce and fiery, taking her breath away. He kissed her so deeply they were both left shuddering.

"I willed you to come to me."

"I couldn't stay away."

All further words trailed away. She let herself be swept off her feet—totally without effort on his part—and carried to the already turned-back bed, thrilled out of her mind she could be the object of such passion.

"*You* had to come to *me*." He stared down at her with his lion's eyes, his strongly muscled, deeply tanned arms propped on either side of her highly aroused body, its contours clearly visible beneath the thin silk.

"It was a test? Did I do wrong?"

"Why don't I just show you?" The words emerged from deep inside him like a deep, hungry purr.

"Clint, we *know* what are we doing? What it means to me?" She tried to raise herself up on her elbow, but had to fall back. She was so weak. Stripped of all strength by longing.

"I do know," he confirmed. "I know you haven't done anything like this before. But we're doing what I've been wanting to do since I first laid eyes on you, my ice princess." As he spoke he was stripping off his white dress shirt, pitching it unerringly onto a chair.

"And what about tomorrow? What about our old lives taking us over? Tonight will be perfect but we can't see around corners, can we?"

He laughed deep in his throat. "Throw off your insecurities. You made it to my door. Hang on to that. In any case, I swear to you I'll want you tomorrow. And the next day. And the day after that… Want me to go on?"

"No time. Remember I have to be back in London by October 1."

He groaned, then threw himself onto the bed beside her, turning on his side to stroke back the masses of her shining hair. "You want this, don't you, Olivia?"

She felt the blood rush to her head. "Oh, God, yes!"

"So…we'll take it slowly. I'm not going to do anything you don't want. First I'm going to kiss you through that shimmering silk, then, beautiful as it is, I'm going to take it off you. I want to know every little last detail of you. The tiniest thing. I want to listen to your heart." He lowered the side of his face to her breast.

It was incredibly arousing, sending primal thrusts deep into her.

"It's beating so fast," he murmured, taking the nipple through the silk.

Full sex lay ahead. She couldn't bear to disappoint him.

Call on your newfound powers.

Even her inner voice sounded frantic.

"You're a very beautiful woman, in just the way I like," he breathed. "More, you're a clever woman, a kind and compassionate woman. So many admirable qualities. I need to tell you, you're my ideal."

Oh, God, let it be so!

She lay perfectly still while his hands and his mouth moved down over her with soft brushing and stroking movements. He made her feel so lush, so delectable, it was as though she was inhabiting the body of a different woman. A woman who knew all about inspiring passion. She grew damp with desire. Lying still became impossible. Her legs began to move. Slowly part. At first her lips moved soundlessly, then she began to make little keening sounds, moans that signified her endless yearning.

His powerful bronze torso rose steeply with his every deep breath. He made her sit up like a child, so he could strip off her beautiful silk caftan. His arousal was great. Finally he laid her back, marvelling at the perfection of her woman's body. Her blue eyes were on fire for him. She appeared beyond caring that she was naked. Or she was revelling in it. What was left of her deeply entrenched inhibitions had flown away.

As naked as she, he returned to the bed, his expression exultant. "You can't go back to your room tonight. I won't have it." One hand moved to cup her porcelain breast. "You must stay with me. I want to wake up looking into your desperately…desperately…lovely…face." Each word was accompanied by soft, thrilling brushes to her mouth.

She held his head as he bent to take one rosy erect nipple into his mouth. Suckled it as though it was a delicious berry. His teeth very lightly nipped, causing her one convulsive shudder after another. Her back arched, then arched again. She could have died from the pleasure, excruciating in its intensity. "Tell me you'll stay?" he demanded with great urgency, now fully astride her, like some pagan god.

Her arms rose to lock ecstatically behind his head. "You can keep me here for ever," she said.

Those final weeks were the happiest Olivia had ever known, sharing the life of the man she had come to love—body, heart and mind. Clint's frequent business trips couldn't be put on hold. She understood that. A couple of times he took her with him, once to Darwin for a general meeting of M.A.P.C., of which her father was a shareholder. She had been greeted royally and invited to sit in. Whenever Clint returned home from a trip, even an overnight trip, they made passionate love, more attuned to each other than they thought possible. He even found time to make brief visits to Georgy, carrying some little gift for her, usually a book. Georgy was a great reader.

"It appears Marigole has taken it into her head to visit as well," he told Olivia, his expression concerned. "Poor Marigole. She's never known what she wants. Whatever she had going with Lucas has gone kaput!"

Georgy, in one of her emails, also passed on the message. "Mummy wants me to call her Marigole now. She has come to see me twice. Wonder what she wants?"

What indeed! Happy as she was, Olivia still felt a twinge of alarm.

Clint debated taking her with him to New Guinea, where McAlpine had large property holdings, but in the end decided it was a bit risky. "You're close to returning home. Can't have you catching a bug. Malaria is still a threat."

He was to be gone for three to four days. "I'll wind things up as soon as I can. If I can't take you with me, at least I can take your image with me. It's imprinted on my heart."

The denouement had to come. It came fast. So pulverising a

blow it nearly knocked the breath of life from her. To think it was another email from Georgy. She had smiled in anticipation as she brought up the message. What she saw froze the muscles of her face. No, no, it can't be! She sat there in the grip of paralysis…

> *Dearest Liv,*
> *Great news! Daddy and Mummy have been having reconciliation talks. It seems like we'll be a family again. Mummy admits she was the one at fault. She swears she is going to change. Daddy says…*

She couldn't read the rest. There was a thick grey fog in front of her eyes. She fancied she heard her heart crack.

Reconciliation?

Georgy wouldn't lie to her. Georgy didn't even know about the escalation of their relationship. It hadn't started until Georgy had been back at school. So annihilating was the shock, she couldn't seem to take it in, though her body was quaking and sobs issued from her throat.

This was the man who had told her over and over he loved her? His parting words were etched on her brain.

"When you're back home, Olivia, my love, you must consider very carefully the future." He had gripped her arms in his urgency. "I can't live in England. I need to be here. You're the one who will have to make the sacrifices. For our marriage to succeed, your tie to me must be the strongest tie in your life."

"I marvel you could doubt that for a second," she had said.

He had crushed her to him as if he would never let her go. Her life. Her lover.

Now in his absence…this monstrous betrayal. It beggared belief a man like McAlpine couldn't find the nerve to tell her of a possible reconciliation with his ex-wife.

He has to be doing it for Georgy. He adores her. Parents do extraordinary things to benefit their children at the expense of themselves. Georgy comes first. But why live a double life?

The answer. Men did it all the time.

Bella was right. Men *were* beasts. And that included her father with his one-night stands. When she could work up the strength she would throw some things into a bag and get the hell out. She couldn't remain another day under his roof. The supply plane was due in that afternoon. She could cadge a flight to Darwin, then pick up a flight to where? God, did it matter? Anywhere she could hide her head. Maybe lie down and die.

Singapore was close.

He was known in this part of the world. "Ms Balfour left the hotel about an hour ago, Mr McAlpine," the receptionist at the world-famous Raffles Hotel told him. "I believe she was going shopping."

Shopping? He felt another turbulent wave of grief carrying with it the debris of rage. When he had arrived back to find Olivia gone and Kath distraught, he had to struggle not to bellow his impotence from a cliff top. This was a woman he had thought a *pure* soul. Truth was at the centre of her. Or so he'd thought, poor deluded fool. He had willingly let her into his life, into every aspect of his being. He had totally let down his guard. This wasn't another Marigole. This was a woman he could trust with his life. Wasn't she the woman who had dived in after Georgy into crocodile-infested waters without a thought for her own safety? Could a woman like that feign love? It didn't seem possible, unless she was schizophrenic?

She had left no note. Utterly gutless.

That's not her. It isn't the Olivia you've come to know and love.

"Good as gold one minute, packed and ready to go the next!" Kath's pale face registered her own shock. "Wouldn't tell me a thing, but kissed me goodbye like she loved me. I tell you, Clint, I don't get it!"

And *he* was supposed to?

He took a seat in the foyer. He was prepared to wait for as long as it took. If she thought she was getting away without explanation she had another think coming. It had been a simple enough matter to track her.

Forty minutes later and there she was. Shining hair back to its smooth pleat, but she wore a very pretty summer dress, a wide turquoise belt cinched around her narrow waist. She wasn't carrying any shopping bags. He let her get ahead, moving as graceful as a long-stemmed flower to the bank of lifts. Then he made his move, lithe as a big cat, getting a tight grip on her arm.

"Ms Balfour, what a surprise!"

He thought she was going to faint. He held her while she took good, deep breaths. "Clint, what are you doing here?" She couldn't hide her distress or her massive shock. She didn't look particularly well and he felt a thump of dread. Could she be ill? There were mauve shadows beneath her beautiful, treacherous blue eyes.

"More to the point what are *you* doing here?" he rasped. "No, wait until we're in your room. I might feel like strangling you, but it would never do in the foyer of Raffles."

Behind the closed door he loomed over her, a tall daunting figure. "Right!" he snapped. "Am I losing my mind or are you? When I left you a couple of days ago we were talking marriage. What's happened since? Why the mad flight? God, Olivia, I could *kill* you."

He looked angry enough. "Why don't you?" From being on autopilot, powerful emotions now flooded her body. "You're a liar and a cheat."

And you love him. No matter what.

His eyes flashed a brilliant anger. He looked appalled. "Have a care," he warned.

"You can't deny it." She reached for her handbag. Glittering tears stood in her eyes, but she wouldn't give him the satisfaction of allowing them to fall. "How *could* you, Clint. I trusted you. You had become my world. But you're a lying brute, just like other men."

Every muscle in his powerful body tensed. "What the hell are you talking about?" He was about a beat away from losing it.

"Here, read it. An email from Georgy." She pitched the crunched-up piece of paper at him.

He caught it, scanned it in a second, then lifted his head. "For pity's sake, Olivia, this is utter rubbish." He sounded deeply disappointed in her. "And it's *not* from Georgy."

"More lies? Who's it from, then?" She picked up a silk cushion and hurled it at him, her body language frenzied. It was beyond her understanding. She could still love this man after what he had done to her. No logic to love. No reasoning.

But he's come after you. Why?

She sobered briefly.

Doesn't make sense, does it?

He had sidestepped the flying missile. "Who the hell do you think?" he grated. "Marigole, of course. It's just her style, a malicious ploy to speed you on your way. I wouldn't take Marigole back if she were the last woman standing."

Her legs buckled under her. She sank down on the bed, not knowing what to believe any more. "Marigole? How did Marigole gain access to Georgy's computer?"

He came to sit beside her, the man who had given her all those perfect Judas kisses. "Clearly you don't know Marigole. If there are games to be played, Marigole is first class. How *could* a clever woman like you be fooled so easily? I'm just so angry with you. What sort of man do you think I am? You told me you loved me, yet you condemned me out of hand."

True, Olivia! Shame. Shame. Shame!

She turned her head to stare into his unwavering eyes. He looked tougher, harder, than she had ever seen him. "I never thought Georgy would lie. She didn't know about us. What *used* to be us." She gave a broken laugh.

"She does now. There's a genuine email waiting for you at home. Couldn't you have waited until I got back?" He didn't try to hide his pain.

"You don't understand." She shook her head violently. "I gave my whole self to you. I was at your mercy. I love you, Clint. But when I read that, I hated you. Just as you hated me. I couldn't possibly accept—" she choked on it "—I'd exposed my heart…."

"And *I* hadn't?" His fingers caught her chin.

"I can only say I believed it to be the truth. Now I feel shaken to my very soul. I thought you might be doing it for Georgy. She means so much to you."

"Obviously you don't realise what *you* mean to me." With furious abandon, he pushed her backwards onto the bed, bending over her, a muscle working along his set jaw. "Was the relationship becoming too intense for you?"

"Are you crazy?" She sought to sit up but he held her back. "Don't you get it? I've searched for love all my life. Then like a miracle I fell in love. You've illuminated my days and my nights. I thought you were the one person who saw through all the layers of self-protection to the very heart of me. Without you I felt my life was finished. Why are you here anyway?"

"For God's sake, isn't that obvious?" he exploded, his temper volatile. "I want you back. I refuse to let you go. I refuse the desolation of waking up in the morning without you. I refuse to allow Marigole her little victory." He reached to pull the pins from her hair, ruffling it wildly around her face. His expression, his voice, the glitter in his eyes, betrayed his rocketing desire. Instant arousal at the very sight of her!

"I have to continue on home, Clint," she pleaded. "I have an obligation."

"I know that." His response was terse. Then, like a driven man, he kissed her—not gently, not even with a measure of control. Full-on heat. He kissed her like a man starved of the woman he loved. Kissed her until she thought her heart was going to explode with joy in her chest.

What a fool you were!

Her inner voice was back to chiding her.

"Forgive me?" she begged, the moment she was able.

"It's done!" He let go of his grief and helpless rage. She was where she was supposed to be. In his arms. "I'm coming back with you." He made the decision on the spot. "I'll make the time. I'm not letting you out of my sight." He gathered her up with exquisite strength. "Let me take care of you. Let me love you." He gave a wry twist of a smile. "I'd been debating whether to strangle you. Now I think I'll settle for making love to you instead."

"And I couldn't want for anything more." She was filled with immense fervour. "I'm at peace now. The despair is over. I've been a fool. But you know as well as anyone I've been prone to bouts of insecurity."

"Never with me. Never again," he answered tautly. "We're *all* fools in love. You've had *me* out of my mind and I thought I'd been through an emotional wringer in my time." He held her eyes. "Now, my one and only love, I'm going to get you out of this very pretty dress." He began to unbuckle her turquoise belt.

She arched her back to assist him.

"Are you really going to come back with me?" She felt over the moon at the prospect. To return home with Clint by her side! To show him off! It would make any woman ecstatic.

"I'm not the kind of guy who backs off big decisions," he was saying. "I'm coming with you to England. We're a team. We go together. I'm sure Oscar won't mind. But right now I'm working on making love to you until you scream for help."

"Won't happen." For the first time in days her face blossomed into radiant smiles.

"I haven't started on you yet," he only half joked. "Afterwards I thought we might pay a visit to a jeweller. I'm thinking an engagement ring. The most beautiful ruby they can show us. Ruby for the heart's blood. You know you hold my heart in these lovely, elegant hands." He raised one and then the other, kissing them devoutly, like a white knight of old. "So what do you think?" His brilliant eyes gleamed.

She released a long rapturous breath. "A ruby is perfect! I would adore it. You're too good to me, Clint."

"Well, that's settled!" Exultation was written all over him

"Some nearly forgotten lines of poetry have come back to me. Want to hear them?"

"I want to hear everything you have to say." She pulled him hungrily down to her.

"You probably know it, scholar that you are. I think I've got it right." He turned his marvellous face to her, beginning to quote: "'Nothing in the world is single; / All things by a law divine / In one spirit meet and mingle. / Why not I with thine?'"

The tears flowed freely as Olivia picked up on the lines of her favourite poet, Shelley. How simply beautiful that Clint should think of them! She would *never* forget this moment.

"'And the sunlight clasps the earth…'" She wrapped her arms tightly, lovingly around him. "'And the moonbeams kiss the sea: / What is all this sweet work worth / If thou kiss not me?'"

A tremendous rush of emotion freed Clint of the days of pain. "So let the kissing begin."

It did in earnest while the whole world held its breath.

Unnoticed by either of them, lost among the stars, on the glass-topped table where Olivia had left her ancient crystal, its glorious sparkle dulled over, the stone suddenly began to radiate iridescent beams of blue light.

Unaccountable?

Magic can happen anywhere, at any time.

EPILOGUE

Article in SCOOP Magazine:

This Month's Exclusive!

Splendour in Buckinghamshire...
Patrician Eighteenth-century Balfour Manor...
Oscar Balfour's Brilliant Birthday Bash!

Coverage: Rainbow Beckwith
Photographs: Bobby Berstein

Greetings, greetings, dear readers! Kisses, kisses—both cheeks—hugs, hugs.

What a scoop I have for you this month, so sit back with a cuppa and lap it all up.

The Balfour Black Tie Birthday Extravaganza. Engraved invitations (I kept mine) requested the ladies wear either silver, white or gold. *Bellissimo!* I can report everyone rose splendidly to the occasion. As we were to find out later, the particular palette was to complement the exquisite flower arrangements and the fantastic interior and exterior decorations.

Sumptuous buffet in the historic banqueting hall, enough vintage champers to top up the Thames, great music, romantic strolls in the manor's magnificent gardens, dancing until dawn. Get the picture?

Anyone who is anyone was there. The blue-bloods, the upper crust, the celebrated, the movie stars and current celebs, plus a goodly sprinkle of the gilded international set. Glad it's Oscar and not me footing the bill.

But enough of that! I know what you really want to hear. So here it is, first-hand.

Any of you who earlier in the year were set abuzz by cruel rumours that our very own dazzling Balfours were jinxed should have been so lucky as to receive a priceless invitation. When I received mine, I kid you not, I fell to my knees.

Power host, Oscar, was at his triumphant best, his distinguished face aglow with pleasure and family pride.

You will know from photographs of your Rainbow covering other big social events what a passion I have for fashion, so naturally I went all out on my gown. Glittering gold lace. But no way could I rival the tremendous glamour of the Beautiful Balfour Girls.

What an orchestration was their entry! Everyone gasped and fell about in genuine admiration. Whatever mastermind party planner thought it up is now assured of a full book from hosts and hostesses dead set to impress.

Oscar's beautiful daughters—Olivia, Bella, Zoe, Annie, Sophie, Kat, Emily and Mia; could any father be so blessed?—came on with such dazzle and pizzazz that the two hundred guests gathered in the magnificent black-and-white marble-paved entrance hall burst into spontaneous applause.

Watching proudly was Oscar Balfour with his companion of the evening, the marvellously chic Lady Primrose Howard, while his daughters—"jewels in his crown," as he later said in a wonderfully witty speech—commenced their spellbinding descent of the manor's gloriously romantic grand staircase.

Utterly, utterly gorgeous, dear readers! It should be a tradition.

Olivia, as the eldest, led off. Talk about goddess worship! She wore a gleaming strapless column of white satin embroidered with crystals, pearls and silver thread—a gown so stunning you could pine away and die for it, that's if you could ever manage such a willowy figure!

Following Olivia came her fraternal twin, our fashion icon, Bella, in an amazing asymmetrical gown featuring wide bands of silver and gold silk.

Must tell you before I report another word, I later witnessed a very touching moment between the sisters, lovely to see, that puts paid to any talk of an estrangement. Take it from me, I'm here to derail it. I've never seen two more devoted sisters. And why not? They're twins. For the first time, I noted they're actually very much alike.

Behind the twins, came Kat, Mia and Zoe, all three positively blooming. Pick up any clues, girls? Watch this space.

Sophie and Annie in lovely, lovely extravagant gowns were next in line to make their graceful descent.

Little Oliver also made a fleeting appearance, waving happily at the gathering before being promptly escorted off to bed.

And for the grand finale! Emily, soon to become Princess of the Principality of Santosa. Real live royalty no less. Could anything be more thrilling than a fairy-tale end?

But the real show-stopper of a truly fantastic evening was, as the sisters started their celebratory descent, accompanied by a fanfare of wonderfully sweeping music, they were joined, in turn, from the opposite side of the fabulous art-hung gallery by their strikingly handsome, elegantly attired partners, seemingly from all over the globe!

Let me be the first to tell you—and don't you forget it—we can expect lots of wedding bells to ring out in the near future, so now is the time to renew your subscription to your favourite magazine.

To wave upon wave of delighted applause the Beautiful Balfour Girls, with their deliciously exciting Significant Others, moved down the stairs to join the throng for a round of introductions, Oscar right in the middle of it, loving every moment, his daughters all lit from within with the joy of reunion and their personal happiness that couldn't have been more on show.

This was one of those evenings, dear readers, that forever remains in the memory. I had the greatest time, as did all of Oscar Balfour's honoured guests.

Hot, hot news coming straight off the press: the upcoming engagement of the beautiful Olivia to her partner of the evening, Australian cattle baron and business entrepreneur Clint McAlpine. There's some distant family connection, I understand. Olivia recently returned from an extended stay at Clint's vast outback desert kingdom.

Wow!

At this stage of my reporting life, I think it's fair to say I've never enjoyed a birthday bash more. I'm sure all of us who were there will long cherish the memory.

Until you hear from me again, keeping you, dearest readers, fully in the picture of what goes on at the best places...

Love and XXXXs,
Rainbow Beckwith

Article taken from Celeb *magazine:*

True Love Is Bountiful!

When Greek entrepreneur Nikos Theakis married one of Oscar Balfour's daughters three years ago, no one expected the glamorous couple to settle into family life so enthusiastically. Yet here they are expecting their fourth child in three years!

Wearing blue chequerboard shorts, the deliciously handsome billionaire looked the picture of domestic contentment when he took a barefoot stroll along the beach at his fabulous oceanfront home outside Athens yesterday. Hand in hand with his beautiful half-Italian wife, Mia, Nikos kept a sharp eye on two-year-old twin sons, Ari and Oscar, as they played in the surf, while his year-old daughter, Giulia—the spitting image of her mother—rode contentedly on her father's arm.

Forever the fierce competitor in all aspects of his life, "Nikos aims to beat Oscar Balfour's record of eight children," a close source to Nikos told us yesterday. "He thinks ten is a nice round number to work towards."

With a wife who looks as stunning as Mia does in a skimpy red bikini while sporting a prominent baby bump, who can blame him?

Since marrying Nikos, the beautiful brunette has made quite a name for herself in the fashion industry as a gifted self-taught designer. Nikos, meanwhile, made world headlines recently when he bought out Mario Mattea, the founder of Mattea SPA, to become the major shareholder of the famous Italian sports car manufacturer in a deal purported to be worth £3.5 billion.

Next week the family will be flying into the UK to join

the rest of the Balfour family in Buckinghamshire for the annual Balfour Charity Ball. With an international guest list that reads like *Who's Who* in the business and celebrity world, you can guarantee the chosen charities the ball supports will be rubbing their hands with glee.

Villa Maravilloso

Dear Daddy,

I just wanted to write and tell you how wonderful it was to see you here last weekend and to thank you for your extremely generous christening present. Carlos and I were so glad that you stayed on after everyone else had left and that we were able to have some time alone.

It was great to be able to take that long walk with you, not just to show you the beautiful countryside, but also for the two of us to have a proper talk together—in a way I can never really remember doing before. But then, life here seems to give me the time to do the important things in life. It's one of the things I love about it.

I know you had expressed doubts that I would find happiness living in rural Spain after my somewhat varied (!) metropolitan lifestyle, but I think you were able to see for yourself just how blissfully contented I am here in Andalusia.

Until our chat, I never realised how bitterly you regretted the past, and how you wished you could undo all the mistakes you have made. But we all make mistakes—every single one of us. That's part of what makes us human. It's what has brought us to the place in which we find ourselves, and I don't think either of us would want to be anywhere else. You were simply following your heart, the way we all do. And you have so many amazing things to show for your life.

All your daughters are settled and you are now a proud grandfather many times over! You are remarkably tender with the little ones, and as I watched you hold my own Miguel, I could sense your pride (and relief!) to have another little boy with Balfour blood after so many girls! I can foresee him spending many happy hours with you in the future, although Carlos says to tell you (very sternly!) that he will be supporting a *Spanish* football team.

We both hope you will come out and visit us again (but for longer next time!) and we look forward to seeing you at Sophie's next month.

Miguel sends you a big kiss, and I have enclosed a photo of the two of you sitting on the veranda as the sun is going down. It's gorgeous, isn't it?

Well, take care of yourself, Daddy, and I'll talk to you soon.

With oodles of love,

Your loving daughter, Kat. Xxxxx

P.S. That woman you've been reported dating seems very *young*!

EMILY AND LUIS...

From the Jornal do Santosa, October 3, 2010:

His Majesty's Secret Service!

Months of feverish speculation about the forthcoming Santosan royal wedding came to an abrupt end last night as it emerged that King Luis married his beautiful English fiancée, Emily Balfour, yesterday afternoon in a private, and somewhat spontaneous, ceremony near her family home.

The ancient church in the small village of Balfour, Buckinghamshire, provided the setting for the service, which King Luis apparently arranged at the last minute and without the bride's knowledge, with special permission of the Archbishop of Canterbury. It was attended by the bride's close family—her seven sisters and their partners, all of whom had gathered at their childhood home to celebrate the sixieth birthday of their father, Oscar Balfour, the day before.

The king's private secretary, Tomás Almeida, was one of the few Santosans present at the service. Speaking exclusively to our reporter from the private reception at Balfour Manor last night, he expressed the king's regret for any disappointment the people of Santosa might feel about this most secret and private of royal weddings. "His Majesty felt that coming so soon after the death of his father, King Marcos Fernando, it was not appropriate to have a lavish public celebration. He also knew how much it would mean to Miss Balfour to get married at home, surrounded by her family."

Wearing her late mother's wedding dress—a simple, slim-fitting column of cream satin—Miss Balfour was given away by her father.

As bridesmaid, Princess Luciana wore an apple-green

net skirt and glittery fairy wings which, according to one of the villagers who gathered outside the church, appeared to have come from the sisters' old dressing-up box at Balfour Manor. "The little princess looked a picture and was clearly excited by the occasion," she commented. "We all were. It was so unexpected, but as word got round the whole village came out to wish them well, and I know I wasn't the only one with a tear in my eye. It was a beautiful golden autumn afternoon, with the leaves falling like confetti and the sun shining down on them as they came out of the church. The whole family was together again—smiling, crying, laughing—and Miss Emily looked so lovely that the king couldn't take his eyes off her for a second."

The king and queen are expected to enjoy a long honeymoon in a secret location before returning to Santosa for next month's coronation.

SOPHIE AND MARCO...

Email from Marco Speranza to Oscar Balfour:

Oscar, please could you make excuses for Sophie and me at the party tonight?

Do enjoy yourself and raise a toast, not just to your beautiful daughter, but also your new grandsons, who, like their big sister, decided to put in an early appearance!

Mother and sons are fine. Actually, they are all perfect! Sophie was utterly incredible and so calm... Did I mention that Rafael did not wait until we reached the hospital? He was born in the back seat of the car. My hands are still shaking! Francesco—he has Sophie's eyes—made his entrance on the steps of the hospital.

Keep the sisters away until tomorrow. Sophie needs rest and I need Sophie.

Regards,
Marco

ZOE AND MAX...

As seen in the New York Times "Living" section:

Mr. and Mrs. Max Monroe Announce
the Birth of Baby Boy

John Oscar Monroe, to be known as Jack, was born at Lenox Hill Hospital on the Upper East Side of Manhattan on February 23. Mother and baby are both doing well.

Max Monroe, the baby's father, experienced a tragic accident nearly a year ago, when his plane crashed on Long Island and he suffered nearly complete sight loss. After a brief respite from business, Mr. Monroe returned to investment consulting, and his private firm, Monroe Consulting, has seen incredible new growth in recent months.

Zoe Monroe, née Balfour, and the youngest daughter of Oscar Balfour, was featured heavily in the press last year when the story broke revealing her illegitimacy. Scandal briefly rocked the illustrious family, but has since disappeared almost completely. Since then she has been involved in various charities both in New York and London, and she organized the Midtown Pregnancy Support Center's fundraising gala in December. She is also working towards a university degree in Natural Sciences.

The Monroes divide their time between New York and London, and, according to sources close to the devoted couple, look forward to "many more little Monroes." We extend our warmest wishes to this new family.

The de Salvatore Vineyard, Venice, Italy
10 December, 2010

Hello, Daddy,
Just a brief note—I know what an old traditionalist you are
and hate receiving texts or emails from the family!—to
let you know that Luc's parents would love to come along
with us to stay with you for the Christmas holidays. There
is no way they are going to miss spending Christmas with
Oliver, and with their second grandchild expected in the
New Year, they want to be here—just in case!

They will be writing to you themselves, of course, to
formally accept your invitation, but I just thought I would
give you a heads-up.

Luc sends his love to you and Mummy, as usual. He
also says to get the champagne on ice—the way this baby
is kicking, Luc is sure that he or she is going to be born
sooner rather than later!

See you soon, Daddy.
Lots of love,
Annie

My Family
by Yazlin Al-Rafid, aged 5:

My name is Yazlin. I am five years old. I live in a palace with my mummy and my daddy. My daddy is called Zafiq and he is the Shake. He is tall with black hair. He is very strong and clever. I like it when he tells me stories.

My mummy looks like a princess. Her name is Bella and she has lovely hair. Sometimes she wears sparkly dresses. She is kind and she hugs me. Sometimes she lets me eat chocolate. My daddy thinks he is the one in charge but really it is my mummy. When she wants him to say yes to her, she wears red lipstick. I am going to wear red lipstick when I grow up. The thing my daddy likes best is kissing my mummy. It makes her smile.

My favourite things are drawing and riding my horse. My horse is called Aliya, and her mummy is called Amira and her daddy is called Batal. I like to ride fast. My daddy says I am too much like my mummy.

Every year my mummy and daddy go to the desert. I stay with my Aunt Olivia. Last year when they went to the desert, Mummy got fat. Then my baby brother arrived. He cries a lot. Mummy says he cannot help it because he is a man and men often make a fuss. I like my family.

♦Harlequin *Presents*

Coming Next Month

from **Harlequin Presents® EXTRA.** Available March 8, 2011.

Coming Next Month

from **Harlequin Presents®.** Available March 29, 2011.

REQUEST YOUR FREE BOOKS!

HARLEQUIN *Presents* ®

2 FREE NOVELS PLUS
2 FREE GIFTS!

PASSION
GUARANTEED
SEDUCTION

YES! Please send me 2 FREE Harlequin Presents® novels and my 2 FREE gifts (gifts are worth about $10). After receiving them, if I don't wish to receive any more books, I can return the shipping statement marked "cancel." If I don't cancel, I will receive 6 brand-new novels every month and be billed just $4.05 per book in the U.S. or $4.74 per book in Canada. That's a saving of at least 15% off the cover price! It's quite a bargain! Shipping and handling is just 50¢ per book.* I understand that accepting the 2 free books and gifts places me under no obligation to buy anything. I can always return a shipment and cancel at any time. Even if I never buy another book, the two free books and gifts are mine to keep forever.

106/306 HDN E5M4

Name	(PLEASE PRINT)	

Address		Apt. #

City	State/Prov.	Zip/Postal Code

Signature (if under 18, a parent or guardian must sign)

Mail to the **Harlequin Reader Service:**
IN U.S.A.: P.O. Box 1867, Buffalo, NY 14240-1867
IN CANADA: P.O. Box 609, Fort Erie, Ontario L2A 5X3

Not valid for current subscribers to Harlequin Presents books.

Are you a current subscriber to Harlequin Presents books and want to receive the larger-print edition? Call 1-800-873-8635 today!

* Terms and prices subject to change without notice. Prices do not include applicable taxes. N.Y. residents add applicable sales tax. Canadian residents will be charged applicable provincial taxes and GST. Offer not valid in Quebec. This offer is limited to one order per household. All orders subject to approval. Credit or debit balances in a customer's account(s) may be offset by any other outstanding balance owed by or to the customer. Please allow 4 to 6 weeks for delivery. Offer available while quantities last.

Your Privacy: Harlequin Books is committed to protecting your privacy. Our Privacy Policy is available online at www.eHarlequin.com or upon request from the Reader Service. From time to time we make our lists of customers available to reputable third parties who may have a product or service of interest to you. If you would prefer we not share your name and address, please check here. ☐

Help us get it right—We strive for accurate, respectful and relevant communications. To clarify or modify your communication preferences, visit us at www.ReaderService.com/consumerchoice.

HP10R

Selene wanted nothing to do with the father of her son, Alex; but Aristedes had other plans…that included them.

Read on for an sneak peek from
THE SARANTOS SECRET BABY by Olivia Gates,
available April 2011, only from Harlequin Desire.

"You were right to turn my marriage offer down," Aristedes said.

And Selene found her voice at last, found the words that would not betray the blow he'd dealt her. "Thanks for letting me know. You didn't have to come all the way here, though. You could have just let it go. I left yesterday with the understanding that this case is closed."

Before the hot needles behind her eyes could dissolve into an unforgivable display of stupidity and weakness, she began to close the door.

The door stopped against an immovable object. His flat palm.

"I can't accept that." His voice was low, leashed.

What did her tormentor mean now? Was he ending one game only to start another?

She raised eyes as bruised as her self-respect to his, found nothing there but solemnity and determination.

Before she could voice her confusion, he elaborated. "I never let anything go unless I'm certain it's unworkable. I realize I made you an unworkable offer, and that's why I'm withdrawing it. I'm here to offer something else. A workability study."

She leaned against the door, thankful for its support and partial shield. "Your son and I are not a business venture you can test for feasibility."

His gaze grew deeper, made her feel as if he was trying to delve into her mind, take control of it. "It's actually the other way around. I'm the one who would be tested."

She shook her head. "Why bother? I know—and *you* know—you're not workable. Not with me."

His spectacular eyebrows lowered over eyes she felt were emitting silver hypnosis. "You're right again. Neither you nor I have any reason to believe that isn't the truth. The only truth. It might be best for both you and Alex to never hear from me again, to forget I exist. But then again, maybe not. I'm only asking for the chance for both of us to find out for certain. You believe I'm unworkable in any personal relationship. I've lived my life based on that belief about myself. I never really had reason to question it. But I have one now. In fact, I have two."

Find out what happens in
THE SARANTOS SECRET BABY by Olivia Gates,
available April 2011, only from Harlequin Desire.

HARLEQUIN® HISTORICAL:
Where love is timeless

USA TODAY
BESTSELLING AUTHOR
MARGARET MOORE
INTRODUCES
Highland Heiress

SUED FOR BREACH OF PROMISE!

No sooner does Lady Moira MacMurdaugh breathe a sigh of relief for avoiding a disastrous marriage to Dunbrachie's answer to Casanova than she is served with a lawsuit! By the very man who saved her from a vicious dog attack, no less: solicitor Gordon McHeath. Torn between loyalty for a friend and this beautiful woman who stirs him to ridiculous distraction, Gordon knows he can't have it both ways....

But when sinister forces threaten to upend Lady Moira's world, Gordon simply can't stand idly by and watch her fall!

Available from Harlequin Historical
April 2011

red-hot reads

Sunny, sensual Hawaiian spring break…again!

Three best girlfriends are recapturing an amazing spring-break vacation they had a decade ago.

First on the beach is former attorney and all-around good girl Mia Butterfield. Meeting up with her boyfriend of old is a bust, so she's shocked when her hero turns out to be someone she'd never have expected…

Find out who it is in
SECOND TIME LUCKY
by acclaimed author
Debbi Rawlins

Available from Harlequin Blaze® April 2011

Part of the sensual miniseries,
Spring Break

Part 2: Delicious Do-Over (May)

A ROMANCE FOR EVERY MOOD™

www.eHarlequin.com

HB79607